D1403281

Copyright

Designed and illustrated by C. Carlyle McCullough and Aero Studios.

For My Jenny

Kevin Rayfield McGill

CONTENTS

Prologue • 7

One
The Voice • 9

Two
The Peruvian • 23

Three
Rocky the She-Bully • 39

Four
Prometheus 10,000 • 49

Five
R-5235 • 69

Six
St. Mary's • 87

Seven
Foggy Flight • 100

Eight
Second Stagecoach • 111

Nine
Waterdragons & Obmorcrabs• 119
Ten
Oaths & Agatha • 137
Eleven
A Question For The Road • 147
Twelve
Trackers • 153
Thirteen
Going to a Better Place • 163
Fourteen
The Truth • 179
Fourteen
The Good Life • 199
Fifteen
Mermaids! • 221

Prologue

Sometime in the near future...

Machu Picchu
Peru

Nikolas! *This is your grandfather, Grand. Our city is in trouble. The city of Huron. She needs you.*

A man, who appeared to be in his early sixties with marble white-blond hair and sky-blue eyes, filled Nick's videomail screen.

The ID and timestamp on the videomail message read:

CALLER: GRAND LYONS (GRANDPA)
TIME: 7:10 AM
LOCATION: MACHU PICCHU, PERU

For years I have been searching for a message from Huron. I believe I have found it here, in Machu Picchu, Peru. Now, what I'm about to tell you will be quite unbelievable, but it's true. The city of Huron is in the past, and it's on the Moon. Or as our people call it:

Möon.

That sounds preposterous, I know, but the Lyons family isn't from this future Earth. We travelled through time and space to escape our enemies who were bent on our death. But now some dark force threatens our home, and we must return to her. I believe this ancient message I am about to find is calling for you, Nikolas.

Chapter One
The Voice

Colorado City, Colorado

Steward Nikolas Lyons! The Rones enter the city of Huron at the peril of us all.

"What?" Nick ripped his face from under the machine. The work shed was lined with all sorts of twenty-first century antique motherboards, microwaves, cappuccino machines, and key-making machines.

And none of them could speak.

The Rones lie about their true intent. They enter the city of Huron at the peril of us all.

Nick dropped the nanodriver. He really had heard a voice. More specifically, he'd heard a woman's voice. It couldn't have been his mom. She was out on one of her global shopping trips with his dad, which he'd counted on. She didn't like it when Nick got into their shed and started messing around with the antique electronic devices. Neither did the fire marshal. But he had to finish his machine. It would change everything for him.

The Rones lie about their true intent. They enter the city of Huron at the peril of us all.

"I'm losing my mind," Nick said, wiping his blond hair out of his face. "I can't lose my mind, not yet at least. Finish the machine. Get off this planet. Then I can lose my mind."

In order to finish his machine, Nick had resorted to the Nick Lyons's living-dead power formula: three parts soda, two parts energy drink, and six parts chocolate syrup, chased down with Pepto-Bismol. But that wouldn't cause hallucinations… right?

The Rones lie about their true intent. They enter the city of Huron at the peril of us all.

Nick looked down to his feet. The voice had come from under the floorboards. "Ha, ha, Tim. Funny. I can hear you under there."

The Rones lie about their true intent. They enter the city of Huron at the peril of us all.

He squeezed his eyes shut and opened them again.

"I will not hear voices…. I can't hear voices."

"You seem disturbed, Nick?" said a motherly digital voice. A white box with two multi-purpose arms and the holographic head of a middle-aged woman floated toward him. It was Nick's nannydrone. There had been enough "incidences" involving the blowing up of old tech that the fire marshal insisted Nick's parents post a nannydrone at his side at all times. Didn't help much though. The drone was as dumb as a box of bolts.

Nick found the nanodriver wedged between a crate and the wall. He grabbed it, wiped off the dust and cobwebs, and went back to work.

"Again, why are you disturbed, Nick," the nannydrone said.

"I'm not disturbed. I'm busy." Nick got down to a knee and undid one of the machine's screws with his finger. "Got to finish the machine."

"I believe you are disturbed," the nannydrone said. It extended a multipurpose arm with a small probe. The probe activated its bioscanner, a fan-shaped laser, and shoved it between Nick's face and the machine. The laser swept back and forth, blinding him several times.

"Nick," the nannydrone said. "I ran a full neuroscan, and it says you are not being honest with me. Something has disturbed you. It seems you are experiencing delusions, Nick? Is there anything I can do? How might I make you happy today?"

"Hug a power line." Nick swatted the probe away.

"Please wait while I process your request..." A clock symbol appeared over her face. "I am sorry, Nick Lyons. I cannot perform such a task."

"Of course you can't. Wanna know why? That would actually make me happy."

"Oh dear, Nick. My biorhythm sensors *now* tell me

you have been upset by an unidentified object within this very room."

"Really?" Nick smacked his forehead. "Wonder *who* that could be?"

"I am formulating a solution to your happiness, Nick," the nannydrone explained. "This solution today is brought to you by Pappy's Pudding Fingers. Lick your way to happiness. Due to a decreased level of serotonin in your brain, dilated pupils, and small but noticeable constipation—"

"Gross," Nick said.

"You would be best served by having a Pappy's Pudding Finger. Chocolate."

The nannydrone buzzed to a locked fridge by the bathroom. Its multipurpose hand flipped and inserted a key. As part of an attempt to open another profit stream, the manufacturer, Lifedrone, distributed complimentary Pappy's products with their nannydrones.

"Here is a Pappy's Pudding Finger on a stick. No charge to you." The nannydrone rose to meet him eye-level. It held the Pudding Finger between its fingers. "Enjoy, Nick."

"I don't want it," he said.

Ignoring him, the nannydrone unwrapped the pudding finger and smooshed it to his mouth. "I can order a month's supply whenever you'd like, Nick."

He ducked away. "Stop."

"Lifedrone and Pappy's have joined to offer a special deal just for you, Nick." The nannydrone shadowed him and smooshed the pudding finger to his lips again and again. "Yummy, yummy to the tummy, Nick."

"Dude, seriously." Nick wiped the pudding finger from his cheek.

"See, yummy, Nick," *SMOOSH* came the sound of the nannydrone smashing the Pudding Finger into his cheek. "So yummy." *SMOOSH.* "Yummy, yummy." *SMOOSH. SMOOSH. SMOOSH.*

"I don't have time for this," Nick smacked the nannydrone's arm. "I have a demonstration this afternoon. The machine isn't ready. Tim's disappeared as usual, and I'm hearing voices. So. Get. Out. Of. My. Face!"

"But..." The nannydrone lowered the pudding finger slowly, "*everyone* wants a Pappy's Pudding Finger, Nick."

He sighed and said under his voice, "I really need to get off this planet."

The nannydrone floated higher, its anti-grav motors purring as it studied Nick. He knew it was computing some way to get him to taste the pudding finger sample. He could hear the motors move closer, it leaned in slowly, cautiously...

SMOOSH. The pudding finger rammed into his left ear.

"THAT'S IT!" Nick yelled and leapt to his feet. He went over to the nannydrone's mini-fridge and picked it up.

"What are you doing with that mini-fridge, Nick?" the nannydrone said. "It is property of Lifedrone."

He marched to the large window overlooking Hiker's Canyon and said, "Open window." The glass swooshed open. He peered out the window to a fifty-foot drop.

"There are nearly three thousand dollars of Lifedrone's products in the mini-fridge, Nick." The nannydrone put up two concerned plastic arms.

"Yeah, I know," Nick said. "And what's your primary protocol?"

"To observe and protect you, Nick." The nannydrone slowly moved toward the mini-fridge precariously hanging out of the window.

"Wow," Nick said. "That's a total lie. I didn't know drones could lie." He began to tip the mini-fridge over.

"Disengaging deflect program," the nannydrone said. "You are correct, Nick. My primary protocol is to try and sell you low cost snacks at high end prices."

"So if I chuck this over the canyon, you'd have to save it?"

"Yes. I would have to save the Lifedrone produ—"

Nick raised his hand and let the mini-fridge tip over. It tumbled three times in the air.

BANGG!!

The first boulder snapped the door open, flinging Pappy's products into the air.

BANGG!! BANGG!

The second boulder sent the door flying away.

It continued to bang and bounce against the granite boulders until a pine tree stopped it.

The nannydrone lit its propulsions and flew out the window with arms outstretched. For a moment, it actually crested into the air, but Nick knew that while Lifedrone had installed their machines with many of the latest flight technologies, one technology it had not bothered to develop was the anti-gravitation system. It could only hover at five feet. Hiker's canyon was fifty-five feet.

The nannydrone fell like a piano.

WHEEEBOOM!! It blew up on impact.

Nick smiled as he watched the drone's battery pack explode into a greenish ball of flame. A pyrodrone launched from some nearby stoop, its hoses aiming toward the flames.

He felt a little tinge of guilt as the nannydrone's plastic skin began to melt into the pine needles. This one had lasted the longest, three weeks at least, but he consoled himself knowing Lifedrone would send over a replacement by this time tomorrow. Pappy's Pudding Fingers won't sell themselves, after all.

The Rones lie about their true intent. They enter the city of Huron at the peril of us all.

"Seriously!' Nick yelled at the wall. "Who *is* that? I don't have time for this. I'm trying to get some work done here."

Nick wasn't usually this grumpy, but he hadn't slept for forty-eight hours, had drunk his weight in chocolate syrup and Pepto-Bismol, and was on his last chance to get off this planet. Now wasn't the time for hallucinations. He had to give every ounce of his focus to the machine.

Nick looked down to the scuba diving goggles, which served as a sort of viewer into the machine. He started to wonder if, in fact, it was his machine, the Prometheus 10,000, that was speaking to him. Maybe it was picking up one of those old-timey radio signals? Which was weird since they were banned in the late 21st century.

He crouched down to Prometheus 10,000 to see if there were any exposed wires. The machine's skin had been stitched together from a theater spotlight, an unwary antique television, and three different game consoles. One could see lights blinking deep within its belly, while cables escaped from various holes only to be dragged back in. His brother, Tim, often referred to it as the greatest abuse of technology. To Nick, it was the machine that would finally get him and his friends off this planet.

Earth.

He wanted to go to Moon. He'd never been there himself. But still, he knew that it was home. He'd watched every holoexplorer video and collected every single movie about it. The shed's walls were lined with screen posters that showed real time views of Moon's craters and outposts. He could imagine roaming around the craters for miles on the Moonbuggy without being tracked by every drone in the area. He heard that Moon teachers actually taught you useful stuff, like how to fix a leaking space suit, or how to filter your own water using Moondust and old oxygen masks. And people shared everything. Food. Clothes. Land. You had to. It was the frontier of space after all. He couldn't think of a better place for him and his friends to start a new life.

Especially after his family's last Christmas vacation.

They were deboarding one of the sonicplanes, returning from a ski trip in the Himalayas. Gate F10 dumped them out into a horde of shoppers, all clutching their newly purchased merchandise. At first Nick didn't know what he was looking at. He assumed someone had unknowingly dropped clothes out of their luggage until he saw those brown eyes and dark skin. A teenage boy from the refugee camp was hemorrhaging. It was his best friend:

Jermaine Coltman.

Nick had met Jermaine Coltman at one of Weaver High's track meets. Jermaine smoked him, no question. Nick admired that a refugee, who was clearly malnourished and underfed, kicked his tail. They'd been friends ever since. Now, he lay on the airport carpet, shaking and sweating.

From nowhere, an ambudrone flew past Nick, announcing, "Geneva virus detected. Geneva virus detected." It aimed a hose at Jermaine and smothered him in quarantine jelly, leaving him there like some dying cocoon. The shoppers, with their department store bags and eyes in perfect balance, stepped beside him, around him, over him. But their eyes never fell on him.

Nick dropped his backpack, tore through the crowd and kneeled down to Jermaine. He didn't know it was the Geneva virus at the time. All he knew was that he needed medical attention *now*. He screamed at the top of his lungs, "Help! Somebody help him! Call 911!" The course of shoppers slowed as they searched for the teenage boy's call for help. When the source was found, they glared at him, glowered at him, a few even shushed him, but no one helped him. A few did mumble, "Ugh. Why they let refugees in here I do not know." "All those kids are diseased." "You can't help them, anyway."

Not knowing what to do next, Nick reached out to the jelly. Suddenly, there was a flash of light, and he found himself laying ten feet from Jermaine, stiff as a board.

He'd been tazed by the ambudrone, and it now floated above him. The white, orbish body, held up a wagging finger, "Please keep your voice down. You are disturbing the shoppers. Besides, he's just a refugee, you know."

They didn't shut down the shopping center—that would be ridiculous after all. I mean, how could one rob the businesses and consumers of their goods and services for one sick refugee kid? Nick knew that the ambudrone, run by its large corporate servers, assessed the value of a dying refugee in light of the financial loss of the businesses in the airport, and chose the businesses. The drone simply roped off Nick's family and shoppers from the quarantined area so they could continue on with their shopping.

Still frozen by the tazer, Nick couldn't move his head, not even his eyes. All he could do was lie there and, at the edge of his vision, watch his best friend shake fitfully, and then intermittently, and then not at all.

Jermaine died in Nick's peripheral vision.

Looking up at the plastic outline of the ambudrone, he had only one thought from that day forward: *I'm getting off this planet. And I'm taking my friends with me.*

Nick sighed. He wanted to get away. It wasn't crazy there, on Moon. If someone is dying, you help them. Why is that so complicated? Everything there was black and white. Everything there was...

"Simple." Nick blinked and shook his head. "Talking to myself now."

So when the wealthy philanthropist, Rick Killings, announced that he would award one billion dollars to the person who could build a machine to return solar radiation to Earth's surface, Nick had found a way to get his refugee friends off this planet. Like some global cataract, a thin cloud covered the Earth, blocking the sunlight for nearly one hundred years. All he had to do was build his solar transference machine, the Prometheus 10,000, and win the "Light The World" cash prize. Then he could afford to buy one-way transworld shuttle tickets for him and his friends to the Trafalgar Lunar outpost. And maybe even purchase a plot of colonial land at Sector 9. Southside of Moon. Easy.

Just like the movies.

Some might call Nick naïve, simple, even a delusional fourteen-year-old—they usually did—but he didn't care. He believed with all his heart that this machine would save his friends. Speaking of, he needed to get his butt in gear if he was going to be ready for the demonstration at two o'clock that afternoon.

The Rones lie about their true intent. They enter the city of Huron at the peril of us all.

"Tim? Is that you? Seriously. I'm gonna punch you in the mouth if you don't knock it off... Tim??"

Come to think of it, Nick hadn't seen his brother all afternoon. He walked to the window overlooking Hiker's Canyon, scanning for any signs of his brother.

A hoverbus swept past their house and toward the refugee camps. The sound of the anti-grav engines made him drop his gaze down to the bottom of Hiker's Canyon. There lay a blond, curly-headed boy, clutching his stomach while trying to cough up a spleen or two. A large teenager hovered over the curly-headed boy, taunting and laughing.

"Oh boy," Nick said. He had found his brother, Tim. And *so* had Rocky the She-Bully.

"You should know better, Tim." Nick bolted out the door. "Never go down to the canyon by yourself... Back off, Rocky!"

Can you hear me, Steward? The woman pleaded. *The Rones lie about their true intent! They enter the city of Huron at the peril of us all! Can you hear me, Nikolas?*

Nikolas! This is your grandfather, Grand, again. I wanted to leave one last message before I went down to the archeological site.

Nikolas's grandfather looked quickly out a car window. He was sitting in the cab of a small hovertruck, a hundred feet off the ground. Below him was the ancient Peruvian site, Machu Picchu. Several work tents were set up next to freshly dug holes.

The ID and timestamp on the videomail message read:

CALLER: GRAND LYONS (GRANDPA)
TIME: 7:32 AM
LOCATION: MACHU PICCHU, PERU

I haven't been honest with you about my activities. I am posing as a project leader at Machu Picchu. Currently I'm leading a team of archeologists to find the oldest artifact on the planet. They believe they're looking for an ancient native weapon. In fact, it's a message. If you watched my last videomail, then you know I am on the verge of finding a message from Ludwig The Toymaker, who sits on the city council of Huron. I believe Huron is in peril, and Ludwig is calling us home, calling you home…

Grand hesitated for a second, gasped, and then shouted out the window, *He found it! The Peruvian found the message! Sorry, Nikolas, but I must go. You and Tim need to pack your bags. By the end of the week we'll be travelling through time and space to Möon and the city of Huron.*

The cradle of all magical civilization.

The screen flickered to black.

Kevin Rayfield McGill

Chapter Two
The Peruvian

Machu Picchu, Peru

Tink. Tink.

Hollow... metal? The Peruvian man squeezed the shovel and tapped the dirt again. *Tink. Tink. Tink.*

He threw the shovel aside. He knew what he was *supposed* to do next. First, as a good archaeologist, he was to report to the project leader his find. Then he was to begin the tedious work of gently removing the dirt away from the artifact with a soft brush for the next three days.

He did neither.

He clawed the ground. Bits of rock shoved under his fingernails. Dirt flew into nose, teeth, and eyes.

They gave up on the western site. Said I was an idiot, he thought, laughing to himself. *Yes, yes. Cigar-shaped, self-emanating alloy, just as he told me. And here it is— the oldest artifact on the planet.*

With one inhale, he blew. He let out a small gasp. There was an engraving, and it said:

Read Me

Read Me? Is that English? That can't be English. This artifact is over ten thousand years old. Long before the English language was around. Is this some kind of joke? He glanced over his shoulder. *Only the ruins of Machu Picchu peered back at the twenty-foot hole.* "Ha!" He congratulated himself. *English? Chinese? What do I care? Oldest artifact ever to be discovered, and I made the find. That project leader told me it would be worth more money than these Peruvian eyes had ever seen.*

The idea swelled before he could stop it.

I could slip it into my pocket. Sneak out after nightfall. And I know just the buyer. The Peruvian loosened his pocket as he parted the object from its archaeological grave.

A shadow passed over.

He leapt to his feet. *What is he doing down here?*

There stood the crazy old project leader with his straw white hair and green trench coat. He never came groundside, preferring to stay in his hovertruck 24/7 to watch over the Machu Picchu dig like some Norse god of archaeology. What the Peruvian didn't know was the old man was Grand Lyons, posing as the project leader of an archeological dig.

"I—I think we've found it," the Peruvian said regretfully.

"Yes. I saw it from the truck. Bring it here, quickly now," Grand barked in a thick, foreign accent.

The Peruvian obeyed. He tapped the *UP* symbol on the auto-lift. Electromagnetic thrusters raised him twenty feet and eye level with the project leader. But he didn't make eye contact with the old man; he *couldn't* make eye contact with the old man.

The project leader frightened him.

No other way to put it. He was abnormally tall with the beard of a wild man and a temper to match. And he used big words like "forsooth" and "malcontent."

With a sigh, the Peruvian surrendered the oldest artifact on the planet into the old man's dirt-trailed hands.

I'm an idiot. Weak, stupid idiot, he thought.

Grand withdrew a monocle and, for the first time ever, smiled, saying, "Read me."

The Peruvian smiled back. "Wonder if the Smithsonian has my Friendbank address. You know, for follow-up questions."

Or a job promotion? He thought. *Maybe even director? I suppose I should hire a publicist.*

With the artifact cupped in his hand, the project leader raised his chest and spit.

"Ugh." The Peruvian covered his mouth.

He rubbed the artifact, spit again, and then scratched it with blackened nails. The Peruvian dug through his back pocket and offered up a bottle of hand sanitizer.

Grand ignored him. "Very good, Ludwig, very good. Couldn't have made the clue more difficult to find. You and your puzzles."

"It—it is quite strange," said the Peruvian. "This script, it is English, yes? Definitely not Incan."

Grand's face rounded on the object. "And why should it be? Laid here when Peru was nothing more than an ice sheet."

A stick cracked in the distance. In one motion, the project leader shoved the artifact into his coat, reached behind his neck, and unsheathed an axe.

"Woah." The Peruvian scrambled backward. "What? *What?*"

He traced a figure eight with the axe head. The jungle responded in silence. The axe was mysteriously hidden again.

"Wh—why do you have a battle axe at the dig... at all?" The Peruvian cocked his head. "And where do you keep that thing?"

Grand curled both fists around the artifact.

Snap.

He broke it in two.

"Are you crazy?" The Peruvian grabbed his hair. The oldest artifact in human history and he broke it like a twig.

The artifact released tendrils of yellow dust. A breeze

swept most of it away, leaving a trace of letters behind.

"I, um, I..." the Peruvian mumbled.

"It's stardust. Now be quiet."

Mr. Lyons,

The Merfolk are in grave danger and in need of their steward, your grandson Nikolas Lyons. Return him home to Möon without delay. I have come to learn of the Merfolk's danger through one of my spies: a wallfly. Watch the memory-in-a-bottle and the wallfly.

You will understand all.

Ludwig, Master Toymaker

"Memory-in-a-bottle and the wallfly?" Grand said to himself. "I don't see the—ah! There you are." He moved away a bit of straw and lifted up a green bottle. Then he pulled out a small vial. He untwisted the vial's top and a mechanical fly fell out. It looked to be made of tin.

"That'd be the wallfly." He held it up to his eye, inspecting it. "Now tell me what memory are you holding, you little bugger? What evil thing gives chase to the Merfolk?" He dropped the mechanical bug into the bottle, and a light flashed.

A scene appeared inside the bottle. It was a miniature version of a man driving a stagecoach along some unknown seacoast. Squinting, Grand put the bottle's mouth to his eyeball. Immediately he yipped and then yelled, "They almost got you there!" A minute passed, and he shook his head, growling some indiscernible word. He shouted again, "Oh, that's terrible!"

Watching the project leader respond to a hidden scene only frustrated the Peruvian. He felt like he was at the theater being forced to keep his back to some really good movie while the rest of the audience went on enjoying themselves.

The Peruvian plopped down onto a lone rock, suspecting that he would be awhile. He was right. Grand kept his eyeball glued to the memory-in-a-bottle for the next three hours. On and on, he yowled and tisked, gasped and shook his head.

Finally, he pulled the bottle away from his face, looked around dizzily and announced, "Doomed! All of them. The Merfolk have been attacked! That's it then. I left her exposed.... I should return Nikolas. I must return Nikolas... but the trackers? Take Nikolas through the timeway, and in so doing, abandon the trackers to this timeline. Kill two birds with one stone." He squeezed his palms. "Oh Huron, what is the way? What is the way? Confound it all! Why is the city quiet?" He locked eyes with the Peruvian. "Why will the woman not speak to me?"

"Women." The Peruvian shrugged back. "Take it from personal experience. They never call back. You just have to move on."

Grand's eyes searched the Peruvian's for a moment.

"Aagh." He waved him off and pulled out the artifact. "Is that all you have for me, Ludwig?" He shook the artifact and more stardust appeared, reading:

P.S. I left a few instruments to aid your journey home. First, a chronostone. It will open up a timeway so that you may return. Use it to bring Nikolas back. You should arrive on Augustist 12th, year 4570 of the 5th Epoch—the very day I have written this.

Second. I have included the steward's horn that Nikolas may speak to the city of Huron. I pray it still functions by the time you arrive. But more importantly, I pray the voice of Huron speaks to him.

To the horror of everyone looking on, Grand took a shovel and began digging at the earth like a butcher gutting an animal. Cries of disbelief came from all around.

Within minutes, he had retrieved a second wooden box. He opened it, pulled out a large stone, and mumbled to himself, "Timeway key. That'll get us home."

He dug for another few minutes until he found a wooden case. He mumbled again, "Steward's horn. Nikolas will be able to talk to Huron. Give us further directions. Further directions is what we need!"

He opened the wooden case. Its brass hinges cried from thousands of years of disuse. It revealed an old phonograph with a large horn and a place to lay a vinyl record.

The Peruvian started to feel dizzy and his thoughts were knotted with confusion and bewilderment.

Phonographs were from the early twentieth century.

That was almost two hundred years ago.

But this archaeological site is thousands of years old. Way before phonographs were invented!

WHAT IS GOING ON!

He saw that strange, green memory-in-a-bottle sitting there, most likely holding all the answers to his questions. Without giving it a second thought, he grabbed it and put it to his eye, just like the project leader had done. Instantly he found himself looking at a set of piranha teeth surrounded by thousands of red eyes chasing a merman wearing mechanical legs.

"Aiihh!" The Peruvian screamed, throwing the bottle down. "What was that?!"

"The evil monster that's hunting the Merfolk," Grand answered. "I must bring my grandson home. He's the only one who can save them." He patted his hands together, nodded, and said to the archaeological team, "That'll about do it. I have tarried long enough. Must find Steward Nikolas Lyons now. Good day to you all." Without another word, he marched to his yellow hovertruck, which was as swarthy and beat-up as he.

"Wait." The Peruvian moved between two team members at the water station. "You're going to do what—who? Are you not this—this Steward Nikolas Lyons? For years you've demanded we call you Mr. Steward Lyons."

Grand looked at the Peruvian with his blazing green

eyes, making him feel six feet short of his five foot ten. "I was! Huron knows that I was. Steward Nikolas Lyons the 11th. But now I must find Steward Nikolas Lyons the 12th, my grandson."

He heaved into the truck. A harness responded to the presence of a body and unspooled itself. With a slam of the door, he nodded an empty salutation to the crowd and pressed the power *ON* symbol. An electromagnetic buzz came from the hovertruck, and it began to lift.

The Peruvian stared at his own stunned reflection in the hovertruck window. The scene was fizzling away like a bad radio signal. He looked down to two empty hands. The artifact that would make him wildly rich currently sat in the passenger seat with a crazy project leader who needed to find his grandson and save the Merrows.

"What's a Merrow?" The Peruvian said to himself. "Wait! You can't leave!" He leapt to the hovertruck, grabbed the door handle, and yanked it open. The hovertruck pitched to the left, forcing Grand to prop one hand on the roof while gripping the steering column.

"Are you mad?" yelled Grand.

"The artifact. You have the artifact!"

"I cannot waste my time in parlay with you. The Merrows, sir. The Merrows are in need of salvation. Now let go before you pitch the hover over!"

"Merrows? What are you talking about?"

"Merrows," Grand shouted over the hovertruck's

whining stabilizers. "Mermaids! Merfolk! Whatever you folks call 'em. They are under the citizenship of Huron and in need of help. If they are to be saved, I must have access to the voice of Huron. I may access the voice through my grandson, Nikolas. Therefore, I must return him to his proper time in history. In short, good day, sir!" He wrenched the car door away.

The hovertruck kicked a foot, and then twenty, into the air.

"Hey... HEY! The grant? You have the artifact! What am I to tell the endowment board?" He punched the air. "Crazy old man!"

The hovertruck stopped its ascent, and the driver's window rolled down. He tossed the silver casing to the ground and leaned his head out of the window. "Oh, and if three monstrous creatures suddenly appear looking for me... run!"

He rolled up his window, pointed the hovertruck grill northward, and launched into the clouds.

"Monstrous creatures... ?" the Peruvian said slowly.

"Told you that guy was a nut." A voice came from the onlookers.

The Peruvian scanned the ground and found the silver casing. He toddled toward it, clutched it to his chest, and bolted toward a stack of empty briefcases. Finding one, he dropped to the ground and stuffed the artifact into it. With a few taps, the password was set. He wasn't going to let it out of his sight again.

A llama cried from the outer perimeter. Its bottom

lip lolled back and forth as it galloped past.

Cliiiiink, tiiiiink. Cliiiiiink, tiiiiink came the sound of grinding chains, escorted by canine growls. Three shadows emerged from the jungle.

The Peruvian wobbled to his feet. "Now wha—?" His voice trailed off. "Heaven help us."

What he saw next utterly convinced him that it was time to retire from archaeology and accept his brother Felipe's open invitation to start a line of clothing apparel for small dogs. That is, if he could manage to survive the next five minutes. Three animals lumbered across the site. And they definitely fit the bill of the project leader's description: monstrous. It looked like someone had taken the head of a hyena, stuck it onto the neck of an ostrich, and stitched it to the body of a raptor.

For a second, the Peruvian thought that they were the same monsters he had seen in the memory-in-a-bottle, but these monsters didn't have the teeth of a piranha or thousands of red eyes. Completely different.

He reminded himself that it was important to not get his monstrous creatures mixed up.

One of the creatures, which had bits of chain criss-crossing its torso, stopped at the hole where the Peruvian had first discovered the artifact. Its neck dropped to the ground while oily eyes stayed on the archaeological team.

Grung, grung, grung, grung, grung, grung came guttural sniffs from the bottom of its neck. The Peruvian's lip curled in disgust. Instead of nostrils at the end of its face, this creature's nostrils were on the bottom side of its throat. It stopped and rose up on two hind legs. Membranous skin whipped open from behind both ears while its head moved around like some prehistoric satellite dish.

The creature found him.

Reegh!

The Peruvian scrambled for the closest hovertruck. Sounds of clattering chains moved toward him. He reached for the handle. It was locked. Claws grabbed at his back and forced him down. He flipped over and found himself looking back at a canine mouth. It opened, revealing teeth for gutting set in a jaw for tearing. He heard his own machine gun breath. The creature's neck slithered over until the two neck nostrils found his face. The nostrils flared, sniffed, growled, and then sniffed unsatisfied. It turned to the briefcase in his shaking hand.

Grrrrh.

The creature's gaze returned to the Peruvian. Its bottom jaw unhinged with serpentine ease. Between rows of teeth pulsed a tubular, pink throat. He closed his eyes for what he knew would be the last time in his life.

"Ooh," he moaned.

Wet lips brushed his hand.

It ripped his briefcase away. Sliding in with fits and starts, the creature's head jerked back several times until the briefcase disappeared down its hungry throat.

The Peruvian sighed. The artifact, which would

make him wildly rich, now lay in the belly of that monster.

The membrane fans folded behind the creature's head, and it looked back at the other two who were currently investigating their own team members.

Schreeg-gah! It commanded them. In a gravelly voice, it said, "After five long years, I have picked up the Lyons boy's scent. We know where he lives. His grandfather is going to fetch him. We must get there first at all cost! Our master wants the boy alive!"

In one strange movement, all the heads lifted northward and in the direction of Grand.

And just like that, they marched away.

The Peruvian rolled over. He watched the tip of the last creature's tail disappear into the jungle. What were they? He recalled the trackers that Ludwig had written about in his stardust letter. The project leader had been on the run from them for a long time.

He shook his head and thought, *Project leader leaves babbling about his grandson saving some mermaids? Says he needs to fetch Nikolas and bring him to his true home? Monsters attack the site? Attack me? It swallows the oldest artifact on the planet and my future in archaeology with it? The only way for me to get it back is to hunt that creature down and gut the artifact from its monstrous stomach? I'd have to be a... hero?*

The Peruvian knew what he must to do.

He tapped the inside of his eardrum.

A voice answered, "Communication One. How

may I connect you?"

"Felipe Sánchez, please."

"Connecting..."

"Aló?"

"Felipe..."

The Peruvian retired from archaeology and became a moderately successful producer of scarves and leggings for toy Chihuahuas.

And never again did he have to worry about a hyena-faced monster and some crazy old man talking about the Steward of Huron, Nikolas Lyons.

I was right, Nikolas! Huron's citizens, the Merrows are in grave danger. I saw it for myself! Grand held up the green memory-in-a-bottle, waving it around anxiously. The Machu Picchu archaeological site could be seen to the left of his dirt-filled cheek.

The ID and timestamp on Nick's videomail message read:

CALLER: GRAND LYONS (GRANDPA)
TIME: 9:32 AM
LOCATION: MACHU PICCHU, PERU

You must think I sound ins—ne. Hope yo—get my message. I'm not getting a good recept—. Pass— through a solar-mining field. Just got back from an archaeological dig at Machu Picchu. I disguised myself as a project leader and have spent years searching from a message from home... your home... our home. I got the message!

Grand lifted up the bottle again, while clutching the

steering wheel. *The Merrows are under attack! Oh. You probably don't know what a Merrow is. Merfolk... You know. Half human, half-fish. They will be wiped out soon if I don't return you to your time and place in history. Look. This is hard to explain. Trust me. When you watch the memory-in-a-bottle, you'll understand everything.*

Grand held the bottle in the video screen, shaking it with every punctuation.

They need you! The Merfolk need you—the Merfolk on Möon!

Kevin Rayfield McGill

Chapter Three
Rocky the She-Bully

Colorado City, Colorado

"Hope Tim wasn't stupid enough to actually attempt a conversation with Rocky the She-Bully," Nick mumbled to himself as he raced down the wooden steps to Hiker's Canyon. The canyon was a large, dry creek bed that separated the massive, newly built homes from the refugee camp and its shanties and dorms and teenagers. The Geneva virus, also known as the genetic plague, had swept across Earth nearly twenty years ago. It attacked the nervous system, killing the adults but crippling the children. By the end of it all, it left millions of children homeless. Local orphanages were unable to deal with the demands, forcing the countries to form their own intranational refugee camps.

Nick couldn't have felt luckier.

Moving next to the camp was Earth's saving grace. He couldn't stand all the kids at the private school. They were snobbish, preppie students. But refugee kids? They knew how to have a good time. Tough as nails and wouldn't say no to anything.

Unfortunately the refugee kids didn't like Tim very much, other than as an opportunity to pound his face in.

"I said leave Tim alone!" Nick yelled to a six-foot-tall, fourteen-year-old—well, girl, if he were to be categorical about it. In a stroke of prophetic naming, her parents had named her "Rocky." Shortly thereafter, they passed away from the virus. The refugee kids ordained her with the full title, "Rocky the She-Bully." With this in mind, Nick made a quick, confident assessment.

Tim's digestive system wouldn't survive the afternoon.

"Rocky!" Nick yelled again as he jumped several steps and landed in packed dirt.

"I can—take—her, Nick," Tim said, trying to stand, but his legs were matchsticks. "Go away! I don't need your help."

Rocky shoved him down.

"Leave him alone," Nick said.

"No, Nick—khaa—khaa!" Tim clutched his pant legs, letting out another round of coughs. "You promised."

"I can help." Nick leaned around Rocky.

"Go away! I *said* I don't need your help."

Nothing could have been farther from the truth. Nick had been protecting Tim since kindergarten.

"Look, everyone," Rocky said. "Tim's big brother's come to the rescue, again."

"*Little* brother," Tim said, trying to stand up again. "Nick's the little brother. I'm the oldest."

"By twenty-eight minutes," Nick said. "We're fraternal."

Rocky's porpoise-shaped neck swung around. She critiqued Tim's floppy physique, dusty, blond hair and sloping brow. Even though he was fourteen, Tim wasn't much taller than a seventh grader. He even had small hands and slow reflexes, like their mom.

Rocky's unibrow led the way back to Nick. He was tall and stocky with large hands, more like their grandfather, Grand.

An unearthly sound came from deep within Rocky. It proved to be a laugh. "Hah, hah, haaaaah!" Her finger pointed at Tim. "*Tim's* the big brother! Oh, that's funny! Ha ha ha! Ha ha ha! You're like Nick's genetic fart."

The hecklers roared at that one.

"Shut your drain," Nick gritted through clenched teeth.

Rocky's mouth clapped shut, sucking up the heckler's laughs with it. Her horse-like legs pushed her forward.

"Out of the way, Rocky," Nick said, trying to step around her, but she shadowed him until they were facing each other, neck to chin.

His eyes crept upward, and he didn't like what he saw. Either Rocky's hair hadn't been combed for months, or the brush had completely given up, taking an easier job as a street scrubber. Her right piggly hand hung clenched, while her other hand held a Pappy's Pudding Finger, which left her mouth and fingers caked in brownish white cream. From her nose came an inordinate amount of hair, especially for a fourteen-year-old. In fact, she just had an inordinate amount of facial hair altogether.

Nick sighed and said to himself for the second time that day, "I really need to get off this planet."

A spark leapt around a black bracelet on Rocky's wrist. The refugee camps couldn't afford to lose track of a refugee because it would have to answer to BioFarms: producer, buyer and seller of human organs. In order to pay for the cost of the camps, the U.S. government had a contract with the BioFarms Corporation. All refugees and their organs were considered their property until the teenagers' eighteenth birthday. It was an ideal business arrangement for the organ-manufacturing corporation. Mortality rates in the refugee camps were extremely high, and it was bioethically required to pass on one's organs upon death. Since the organ manufacturing company would be upset if they lost a "harvest", most refugees were leashed by black bracelets, unable to wander more than fifteen miles from camp. If they did, their leashes would set off electric shocks, reminding them to return to the perimeter. For the unruly refugees, their leashes were set to three miles.

Rocky's was set to one hundred yards.

Her leash sparked again, making her arm twist.

Nick smirked. "Got you on a short leash?"

"I don't feel it no more." Rocky took a long, drippy lick from her Pappy's Pudding Finger, showing the readout on her leash: *Geneva Virus Levels: 0.05. Chance of Cardiac Arrest: 1 in 100. Life Expectancy: 19.*

A pang of sympathy ran through Nick. Growing up in that refugee camp wasn't an easy life. Maybe she was just misunderstood.

"They shortened her leash again," a bystander said. "Rocky was caught sneaking into a pet shop off of I-90. Mixed all the pet food up with the Geneva virus and fed it to the animals."

Rocky smiled a brown pudding smile.

Nick's sympathies evaporated. "What do you want with Tim?"

"I told him to give me his pudding finger." Rocky curled her lip. "He wouldn't. We don't get any fancy stuff like you *preppies* up there. So what? You gonna hit me now?"

"I'm not supposed to hit a girl. Grand wouldn't like it," Nick said, clearly against his will.

"You won't hit a girl? Oh, look at you," Rocky said.

"Aren't you a goody two-shoes 'cause you won't hit a girl. But the real question is..." Her head bobbed like a buoy. "Who's. The. Girl?"

"You're right. That's a *very* good question."

"Oooh," the hecklers said.

"What? Did? You? Say?" Rocky's eyes grew.

Don't hit her, Nick thought. *Don't hit her. Grand wouldn't like it.*

"Come on, Tim. Let's go." Nick turned toward the house.

"Oh no, you didn't. Where're you going? Is it feeding time for grandpapa?" Rocky rounded her arms imitating an old grandpa. "I need a wipe, *Nicky.* I think some of this plum juice dribbled on my big, fat, belly!"

The hecklers guffawed in response.

Nick turned quickly and took three long paces, cocked his head up and grinned. He smiled so long, Rocky started to get an uncertain look in her eyes. Nick found the smile to be a very useful, versatile instrument in a confrontational situation. Way better than a grimace. It was great for a face-off with knuckle draggers like Rocky. You just smile ear-to-ear, long enough for your opponent to let their guard down. All the while thinking, *I'm about to punch you in the face.*

Like right now, for example.

CRACKK!

Rocky spun, her dreadlocks tilt-a-whirling, while the Pappy's Pudding Finger somersaulted away.

"Don't talk about Grand like that!" Nick said and

then pushed two awestruck kids apart and marched to-ward the house.

"Mggggrrrhh!" came an inhuman sound.

Nick looked back.

"Raaggh!!!" Rocky leapt to her feet and charged. Nick shifted slightly to the left, grabbed her waist, and threw. She fell with the impact of a moderately sized meteor.

"Aaaiiighhh!!!!" Rocky's face turned beet red.

She dug her pudgy fingers into his shoe and pulled. Nick's world spun. The ground kicked air out of his lungs, and the cloudy sky looked back down. She charged on hands and knees. Nick crab walked in re-verse while she lashed at his shins.

"Woah!" He jumped to his feet. "Freak!"

The Rones lie about their true intent. They enter the city of Huron at the peril of us all.

No, no, no, Nick thought. *Come on!*

The Rones lie about their true intent. They enter the city of Huron at the peril of us all.

The voice was so strong that little lightning bolts danced around Nick's view, and vomit swirled at the back of his throat.

The Rones lie about their true intent. They enter the city of Huron at the peril of us all.

Nick's lips started to move, even though it wasn't his voice. "The Rones lie about their true intent. They enter the city of Huron at the peril of us all. The Rones lie about their true intent. They enter the city of Huron at the peril o—"

Rocky's shoulder slammed into stomach, separating organs.

"Oooof!" Nick groaned. He was on the ground again. She grabbed a snatch of his blond hair and dragged him to his feet. Fortunately, she left her right side completely exposed. Nick took full advantage.

Crackk!

Rocky toppled over. Her legs kicked up at eleven o'clock, teetered, and fell to nine.

Nick stood to his feet and prepared for the resurgence.

She said nothing.

Nick heard his own heavy panting. "Grand's awesome. Talk about him like that again, and it's you in traction." In a triumphant breath, he pushed through the crowd and toward the shed.

"Auuiigghhh!" Rocky's scream frightened away a flock of pigeons. "You're not supposed to hit a girl!"

Nick waved his arm to Tim as he passed by. "Demonstration. Two o'clock? What the heck, Tim?! We've only got a couple of hours left. The press might even show up this time."

"I could have taken her." Tim grabbed Nick's arm. "I didn't need your help."

"Whatever, dude," Nick said.

"We made a deal." Tim wiped the caked blood from his nose. "You don't bail me out anymore, and I don't snitch on you about all your little experiments."

"I *so* don't care right now," Nick said. "How am I supposed to finish setting up for the demonstration if you're in the ER fighting for your life?"

"Oh," Tim rolled his eyes. "Now I get it. You didn't care about me at all. This is about your delusions of running away to Moon. Well, I love you too, brother."

"Are we getting off this planet or not?" Nick said. "I thought you were on board with leaving this place?"

Tim straightened his shoulders, paused, then deflected, "What's a Rone?"

"I dunno." Nick looked away.

"You were all psych ward about Rones being bad and babbling on about some city. What did you call it? The city of—"

—*Huron needs you to come home!* Grand declared on Nick's videomail message. The ID and timestamp now read:

CALLER: GRAND LYONS (GRANDPA)
TIME: 12:11 AM
LOCATION: Santorini, Greece.

I haven't heard from you and I'm concerned you're not getting these messages. Apologies if you have received several of them back to back.

I'll be there to pick you and Tim up once I break the scent of these confounded trackers! Those monsters have haunted me for years now. Everything you need to know about the Merfolk is in this memory-in-a-bottle.

Grand tipped the bottle's mouth to the camera.

Once you watch the message for yourself, you'll understand what your dear old grandfather is babbling about. Look, this isn't your home, this future Earth. You are from another land. Another time. You are from the Moon!

Grand leaned into the camera.

But not the Moon you know.

Chapter Four
Prometheus 10,000

Lyons? Did you hear me, Nick Lyons?" Tim said, trying to keep pace with his brother up the canyon steps. "You went crazy back there. Certifiable. How hard did Rocky hit you? You were babbling on about Huron and Rones. They're evil or something."

Swish. The shed door automatically opened.

Nick stopped and sighed, "OK, fine. I keep hearing this, I don't know, voice in my head. Something about a city—I don't know."

Tim stopped. "I totally called it. You *are* crazy. Just took a while to go full blown."

Nick stepped through the shed door.

Beep, beep.

"Welcome, Nick Lyons," Hospitality 3000 fired up. Above the shed door was a cylinder-shaped sensor programmed to recognize and introduce every person that stepped through the doorway. Except this particular one added its own flair.

"Nick," Hospitality 3000 announced. "The believer of all things. Once, when Nick was five years old, he believed with all of his heart that people could fly. More specifically, he believed Tim could fly. So there Nick was, twelve stories high, holding a very scared Tim out of the window. That's when his mother, Sonya Lyons, let out a maternal shriek and lunged for the two brothers. 'In-the-Nick-of-time' became a popular catchphrase in the Lyons' household."

"Giving me flashbacks," Tim groaned. "I hate that thing, Nick. Turn it off."

"Can't," Nick said. "Daniel hid the shut-off switch."

Nick's uber intelligent friend, Daniel, had taken the standard Hospitality 3000 found in most suburban houses and demonized it. Somehow he had figured out how to tap into everyone's social utility sites, email accounts, the Homeland Security system, so he could give what he called "a full and honest representation of the individual."

"Bet you can turn it down." Tim climbed the worktable and swept his hand around the edges.

Swish... swish. The door slid open.

"Entering Caroline Wendell," continued Hospitality 3000. "One of the three Wendell sisters hailing all the way from the refugee camp."

"He-llo," Caroline greeted them in a breathy tone. She wore her usual print flower dress and horn-rimmed glasses, which was steamed up by a ceramic bowl teetering in her clutches. "I made food for the after party. Mashed potatoes."

"People only like Caroline because she can cook from scratch," announced Hospitality 3000.

"I wish we could shut that off, Nikolas," Caroline said.

"A rare commodity in this century. And for only a fourteen-year-old, she is a fantastic cook. Chocolate chip cookies after school, pie on Sundays, and a turkey for Thanksgiving. If boys won't fancy her for her looks, they'll fancy her for her key lime pie."

"The English accent just makes it more insulting," Caroline said.

Swish... swish.

"Entering Brandy Wendell."

"It's so making my hair limp." Brandy held a large, metal platter covered in aluminum foil. "Caroline? Where do you want your murdered cow?"

"Brandy couldn't be more different," Hospitality 3000 continued. "Being the youngest sister, she hates to cook. Brandy claims that it keeps her from her number one love: looking cute. In defense, Brandy also claims that cooking keeps her from talking with her friends, all 2,372 of them to be exact. Some people collect stamps; Brandy collects people."

"Caroline," Brandy said. "Your roast?"

"You made a roast?" Tim said to Caroline.

"Yes I did, Tim. It's a recipe I've been meaning to try." She shoved a non-functioning radio aside and set down the mashed potatoes.

"For the after-party?" Tim said.

Brandy called out, "Caroline? The murdered cow?"

"Next to the other thingamajig," Caroline said.

"Microwave," Nick offered.

"Oh. Is *that* a microwave? Neat," Caroline said, removing her glasses to wipe off the steam.

"Oh. My. Gawsh. The smell of animal death—it's so in my sweater." Brandy plopped the roast down next to the microwave and quickly unbuttoned her cardigan. "OK. Angora. Six thousand dollars off the rack. Not that, you know, I actually paid for it."

"Where you get your clothes is a mystery," Caroline said. "We live in a refugee camp, you know."

"Daniel," Brandy said.

"Where does *he* get your clothes?"

"I don't know. I ask, but his only response is 'I have my sources'. It's all I can get out of that boy. Anyway, it's not like I ask where you get all your roast beef and pies."

"Pies!" Caroline put her hand to forehead. "Oh, dear. I forgot the pies."

"OK, Nick," Brandy said. "I expect a full on promotion to your little inner-sanctum here. Spent all morning getting the word out for your show. Most of them said 'no' to the show, 'cause of the last incident with the burning down of the greenhouse and all, but 'yes' to the after party."

"Demonstration," Nick said.

"What?" Brandy said.

"It's not a show," Nick corrected Brandy, pointing to the machine. "This is a scientific demonstration."

"Yeah," Brandy said. "Whatever. When towers of flame and smoke are involved, it's a show."

"What will I do?" Caroline said. "I need those pies."

Brandy rolled her eyes. "Call Haley and tell her to bring them already."

Clop, clop, clop, came the sounds of wood hitting concrete.

Swish... swish.

"And now, all the way from the refugee camp, half-brothers Daniel and Xanthus Kobayashi," Hospitality 3000 continued its exposé.

Two boys stood in the doorway. One had Japanese features and leaned on a cane; the other was chubby and looked to be half-African, half-Japanese, and wore a pair of holobox virtual reality glasses.

Daniel walked in slowly.

"Twenty-year-old Daniel Kobayashi is not much taller than a hobbit and intelligent beyond his years. By the early age of ten, he had made the front cover of Japan's holopaper, 'I'. They named him "Child Genius of The Year" for discovering the very first non-metal magnet. That was until the genetic plague killed his mother, crippled him, and left him utterly hairless, which makes him more goblin than hobbit, I suppose.

Xanthus saluted Nikolas and flipped up his holobox glasses.

"Xanthus, Daniel's half-brother, is thirteen years old. Xanthus explains to everyone that he received his name from a visit in the night by a tribal leader indigenous to Sub-Sahara, Africa. The African tribal leader is known for his powerful magic and warrior-like skills. This would be true if by 'African tribal leader' he means 'I live in my own fantasy world because I can't cope with life at the refugee camp.' Xanthus's pitiful fauxhawk, earring of a silver woman, and mismatched black outfit make for an awkward compilation and a lack of girlfriends."

Xanthus found a lone barstool, flipped down the holobox glasses again, and announced, "Gotta beat this level, Nick. Let me know when you're about to make ecological history." With that, he was lost to the virtual reality world of *Magicgeddon.*

"Nick," Daniel nodded, his bald cranium reflecting the soft UV light.

"Daniel," Nick nodded back.

Daniel turned an inspecting eye to the room. He began to make his way around. Nerves crept up Nick's back as he watched the boy genius limp to the machine and inspect the Prometheus 10,000 like some five-star general of science, if those even existed.

"Hmm," Daniel said to himself, then moved to the edges of the room where three fishbowls had been placed on wooden chairs. Each bowl had a piece of charred cardboard taped to it with the scribbled numbers *#17, #18,* and *#19.* The bowls were filled with sooty water.

Daniel traced a figure eight in bowl *#17* and then tasted the black water.

A fish eye rose to the surface.

"So, yeah," Nick said. "We couldn't experiment on ourselves. I, uh, I've been testing the re-projected sunlight on the fish. Trying to get the levels right."

Daniel said nothing. He swished the water with his pinky finger. Another eye rose to the top, but this one was attached to a fish paddling desperately.

"Mom and Dad have like a hundred of those fish. They won't miss a few."

Daniel still said nothing.

"Well," Daniel finally spoke, "experimentation is essential to the scientific method."

Nick's shoulders dropped. The boy genius approved.

Swish... swish.

"Entering the oldest of the Wendell sisters, Haley Wendell—"

"I've got pies," Haley said. She stood in full karate gi while holding two pies like a waitress at a small town diner.

"Thank goodness, Haley," Caroline clapped.

"My match went a little long. Sorry, Nick," Haley said. "Then Caroline went all manic about her pies."

"Haley!?" Tim yelled and did a 180°, the motherboard sailing from his hand.

"Tim!" Nick lunged after the motherboard.

"Hi, Haley," Tim's said. "How are you? How's life? Win any state championships? I bet you beat up all those girls. You're like a queen... of kung fu. A—a kung fu queen. Queen fu. Ha. Ha. Ha. Ha. Ha. Ha. Ha." Tim's smile could swallow the Mississippi.

"Hey, Tim," Haley said.

"Great. Thanks for asking, Haley. Um, yeah..." Tim's eyes danced around the room, desperate to hold onto the anemic conversation.

"Sixteen years old," Hospitality 3000 continued, "with enchanting blond hair and deep blue eyes. Haley's name is on the lips of every boy at the refugee camp without any aid on her part. In fact, it takes a brave boy to ask her on a date, knowing that Haley responds with more than a 'no'."

Haley inhaled deeply and turned around. She spotted two old-fashioned milk crates underneath the workbench.

"She verbally assaults would-be suitors," Hospitality 3000 said, "leaving only a scarred psyche behind. Over Christmas break, Weaver High School's basketball team, who had won four state championships in a row and were well on their way to winning for the fifth year straight, made a bet as to whom she would say "yes" to first on the team. Every team member stepped up and took their turn.

"She told them exactly what she thought."

Haley stacked the crates.

"Not only did the basketball team not win state championship that year, the point guard asked to be transferred to another school because, and I quote from his Friendbank account, 'I have serious questions about my own ability to dribble a ball, defend the basket, or lift a fork and put it in my mouth.'"

Haley climbed the crates and faced Hospitality 3000. She looked around the room and locked onto Daniel with her steely blue eyes.

"Now only nerds and misfits dare to ask her on a date, as they are already accustomed to verbal assaults in a public environment. But do not be fooled by her aloof countenance. She is madly in love with—"

"Haa!" Haley executed a perfect half crescent kick, her gaze never moving from Daniel.

The now smoking Hospitality 3000 system swung over the doorframe by a red wire.

CREZAKKK!

The box fell, shooting out a bed of sparks.

Haley jumped down and said to Daniel, "Put it back up, and you'll be trading that cane in for a breath-operated wheelchair."

"So, guess what, Haley," Tim said, leaning against a small bookshelf. "I hit a girl."

"You hit a girl?" Haley spun around.

"I mean... um, yeah, um," Tim's voice cracked. "But it was a tie. You know. Tim: two. Rocky the She-Bully: two." Tim raised his hands, pretending to do a victory dance.

"So, you couldn't win a fight with a girl?" Haley's brow rose.

"No!" Tim's voice cracked again. "I could have—just trying—just didn't want to make her look bad."

"Congratulations," Haley said.

"Thanks!" His voice cracked a third time. Puberty wasn't taking any prisoners.

She inhaled deeply, "That's not what—!"

"I submit to you," Nick cut off the inevitable verbal carnage. "I submit to you the first ever solar battery projector. Thank you all for coming out to the beta test demonstration. While I am disappointed the press didn't show up, I'm sure word-of-mouth will make up for it. Please distribute the protective eyewear, Tim."

Tim pulled out a small box and opened it. The contents looked more like a collection of swimming goggles than protective eyewear. He started passing them around. Snaps of rubber came from around the room as everyone stretched the bands over their head.

"OK. I'm supposed to give a speech at Rick Killing's Light The World Contest," Nick said, "so I'm gonna practice on you guys." His voice dropped an octave, and he raised his chest. "It is common knowledge that Earth's climate has been altered over the last hundred years, leaving us with the Great Cloud and a lack of proper UV radiation. The sun's output is eighty percent less than what it used to be—"

"Three percent less." Daniel corrected him. "If it was eighty percent, we'd be talking to each other through an ice sheet."

"Right," Nick said. "Three percent. That's what I meant. Anyway. Oh. Don't forget the helmets, Tim."

Tim had already shoved a football helmet over his own head and was passing around an army bag.

Brandy reached into the bag and pulled out a helmet. "Aren't these the missing helmets from Weaver High?" she whispered to Caroline.

"Dude," Xanthus grinned at Tim. "What do we need helmets for?" Tim looked back at him long and hard. Xanthus's grin disappeared, and he quickly shoved on the helmet.

"Currently," Nick continued his speech. "Artificial UV lights have been used to compensate for the lack of sunlight, but they're really expensive to maintain and, you know, suck a lot of power. One day I was watching this video on Ned Talk—"

"I love those," Xanthus said under his breath.

"—They were talking about the updated solar batteries in cars. Everyone knows that cars used to run off the old solar batteries until the Great Cloud. They had to redesign the batteries so it could capture as much solar radiation as possible. They took the photovoltaic cells, which converts solar into electricity, and upped their intake by three hundred percent. That got me thinking. What if we didn't convert it to energy fuel for cars? What if we collected up all that solar light flying around in the air, stored it somehow, and then, you know, shot it back out onto cities, highways, houses. We could have sunlight bulbs on the roads and in homes.

As the god, Prometheus, brought fire to humankind, I bring sunlight to the Earth! The Prometheus 10,000!"

Nick shifted to the left, holding his hand out proudly.

"Woohoo!" They all clapped, their football helmets bobbing back and forth.

"Please refresh our memory," Daniel said, muting the applause. Nick knew that Daniel was the smartest person in the state of Colorado. He didn't need his memory refreshed. "What's your plan again? Why are you doing all this?"

Nick raised his hand as if to gesture how obvious his plan should be. "Rick Killings is offering one billion dollars to the first person who can develop a solution for the Great Cloud. You know, to get the sun back. There's so much wasted sunlight out there, above and below the fog. So we'll store it up and send it down to the cities. All I have to do is, you know, invent the machine. Then I get the money, buy a ticket to Moon, and finally leave this planet. Simple."

"Simple?" Daniel cocked his head.

"Yeah," Nick shrugged. "Invent machine. Win

prize. Leave Earth. Simple."

"He wants to move to the Moon," Tim said with a less excited tone. "Start a new life."

"That sounds nice," Caroline perked up.

"Yeah," Haley said. "I'd leave if I could."

"Good." Nick's smile disappeared. "Cause that's why I'm doing this. If I win the prize I'm taking you guys with me. What am I going to do with a billion dollars?"

"Really?" Haley said, standing straighter.

"That's the whole point, Haley. We could have fun up there, in the colonies. Get away from, you know, all of this." Nick nodded out the window to the refugee camp's fence. "You'd come with me, right?"

"Um, I'm pretty sure the answer is 'yes'," Xanthus said. Everyone nodded in agreement except for Daniel. He only leaned on his cane while his head stooped under the weight of the football helmet.

"So," Nick said. "Awesome, right, Daniel? The plan: Build the machine. Win the prize. All go to the moon and live a life of luxury and adventure?"

"I think," Daniel said, "the football helmets were a good choice."

"Good enough for me, then. Now..." Nick bowed proudly. "Let the demonstration commence!" He snapped on rubber gloves, donned a welder's mask, and made a quick hop, grabbing two handgrips.

"Wait," Brandy said. "You've boiled all of your other test cases."

"Not really." He turned the machine toward a lone fish in a glass bowl at the far end of the room. With the monstrous machine pointed in its direction, the fish zigged and zagged desperately. It recalled previous experiments involving the untimely death of its brethren.

"Not again," Brandy said. "That's just evil."

"Are we ready, Tim?" Nick said.

"Sure," Tim said slowly.

"All right, Tim. Now, I think we made a mistake in the field array calibration last time. Needs to be a little more focused." Nick reached around the machine to an odd assortment of knobs. He turned a large silver one, then pulled a rope. A hole appeared from the roof, casting gray light over the machine.

"The solar battery will now take the diffused solar light in the atmosphere," Nick explained, "store it in the machine, and concentrate it on our test subject."

Tim bent down to a car battery and a pair of positive and negative cables. He attached the cables to the battery, took a deep breath, and then pushed the cables into the machine's two holes.

Sknazz. Pop.

The machine's insides began to glow.

"Success!" Nick punched the air.

"Wow," Brandy said. "It really works?"

"Of course," Nick said.

Tim stood up, his face slightly pale. "If by work you mean it didn't blow up in my face and make my nose hair sprinkle out like ground pepper, then OK, it works."

"Muzzle your non-believing tongue, infidel!" Nick raised his hand.

Tim rolled his eyes.

"Now then. The video recorder, Tim. We'll need to record it for the press conference."

Tim ran over and adjusted an old 3D recorder mounted on a tripod.

"Commencing countdown," Nick called out. "Ten. Nine. Eight. Seven. Six. Five. Four. Three. Two. One!" He smacked a red button on the side of the machine.

The room swelled with light. Everyone slowly stepped back to the wall. The machine went dark. They could hear a knob clicking.

"That it, dude?" Xanthus called out from somewhere.

Nick tightened the grips until his knuckles turned white, then planted his left foot behind him like a runner at the starting line. Tim grabbed one of the firmer poles on the wall.

"Not quite. Now, we have to see if the machine can reproject the solar li—"

Crack-pop.

There was a blast of yellow light. A girl's scream. Nick gripped the machine as it began to shake and roar. The fish wiggled furiously.

"I think it's wor—!" Nick looked back to give Tim a thumbs up but stopped.

The shed and everyone in it were gone.

"Uh, guys?"

Nick was standing at a dark crossroad.

"Hey, guys?"

He squinted and saw a ramshackle of houses up and down the road. Behind it was a horizon shrouded in city lights. His nose was bombarded with a rich, organic smell, and he felt cobblestones under his feet. Something flickered at the corner of his eye. He jumped.

There in his right hand was a katana lit in blue fire. He lifted it up to his face and studied the flames as they walked up and down the sword.

"Seriously, what is going on?"

He wanted to raise the sword higher, but his arm felt constricted, like he had on a suit. He looked to his right arm and down his chest. For some reason he was wearing a black wool coat, golden vest, and black pants with black boots. He slowly looked up and found the bill of a hat.

"OK?" Nick said, taking the hat off slowly. It was a bowler hat. "Where am I?"

But for some reason he already knew the answer. *This* was what the voice had been talking about—the city of Huron. And he knew something else too. Huron wasn't on Earth.

It was on Moon.

That was completely ridiculous, of course. Moon was an empty satellite devoid of oxygen and had very little gravity. There were no cities on it, especially ones with cobblestone streets. Still, somewhere past logic and reason, Nick knew this place. He wasn't sure why, but he really *did* know this place—like one's first house or that park your parents would take you to as a little kid.

And then he knew why it felt familiar.

"Home," he said.

The lunar colony was the home he'd always wanted. But there was another home beyond memory. An unknown home. A fantastic home. Huron was that home. Suddenly, he wanted to go to Huron more than anything else in the world. This is where he belonged. But it didn't make sense. There was no city on Moon. Zip. Zilch. Nada.

Huron's voice began to echo from all the windows and doorways. *Keep them from my gates, Nikolas. The Rones bring death to your city!*

"Who are you?" Nick said. "What's going on... ? Hello... ? OK. I'm kind of freaking out here. Is this real? Hello? I can't do this right now. Seriously. If I'm going insane, I'll never get off Earth. They'll lock me up in the loony bin forever. Hello... ?

Nick squinted into the darkness. "Are you there?"

The Rones will destroy your citizens. They will destroy me!

Nick pointed the sword into the darkness, hoping it would give him more light.

"Who are you?"

Please, Steward. Come home, Nikolas. Nikolas. Ni—

"—ick! Nick!" Tim screamed. The vision oiled away and was replaced with Tim waving his hands frantically. "Are you listening, you 'tard!? The beam's too focused. It's cutting through the bowl!"

Nick looked up to see a white-hot beam, no bigger than a pencil, shoot straight through the fishbowl. Small waterfalls began spitting out of the newly burned holes.

"No, no, no, no, no, no." Nick flipped up his welder's mask and yanked open a panel. "Don't worry. I got this."

The fish stared at the growing holes and small waterfalls. It realized what the holes meant: freedom from the horror that was this glass prison. With a new hope, it swam toward the escape route. Nick fiddled with several knobs and turned a blue one.

The fish pushed through the hole.

Nick turned the knob twice. The light bloomed from a beam to a yellow glow.

The fish flipped up, arching and twisting its body. Now encased in the yellow glow of Prometheus 10,000, it flipped its torso skyward.

"Hah!" Nick yelled and twisted a smaller knob. There was the burst of a brilliant white light. Everyone covered their faces.

The fish reached the top of its dive, hovering, posing in the light....

A snowy substance fell to the ground.

Tim ripped off the Weaver football helmet. "Turn it off, Nick!"

Nick reached for the orange power cord and tore it from the wall.

Brandy squealed with arms outstretched, "A tan. Bronze!"

"Nick!" Haley pointed. Where there was once a water

bowl, wooden chair, and a gold fish making its great escape, now swirled a cloud of white ash. And behind the ash, a perfectly cut hole in the shed. And behind the hole, a stunning view of Hiker's Canyon.

On fire.

"Ah! My roast, Nick!" Caroline ran with outstretched arms to the beef-fueled bonfire.

The football helmet fell from Tim's hand as he stared at the burning trees. "We—are—so—dead."

"Post an update for me on Friendbank. I don't have access to Nick's fan page," Brandy yelled into her cell. "Tell everyone the after-party is cancelled.... Yeah, again.... No. Just some trees this time. I know. I know. They're living creatures too...."

ZZZZzzzzz came the sound of pyrodrones zooming across Hiker's canyon, their anti-fire hoses at the ready.

The scene around Nick fell into chaos. Prometheus 10,000 exploded into a bloom of sparks and smoke. Teenage refugees ran around the canyon in horror and pandemonium. Caroline smacked at her roast angrily. But Nick didn't notice any of this. All he could think about was the woman-voice in his head crying out about the city of Huron.

And she called him "Steward Nik—

—olas. This is Grand again. Not sure if you got my last message, but the solar harvest plant above the Mediterranean must have messed up my phone.*

The ID and timestamp read:

CALLER: GRAND LYONS (GRANDPA)
TIME: 2:59 PM
LOCATION: BEIJING, CHINA

I am taking a roundabout way to Colorado. Trying to shake off these trackers!

I must get to your house before they do. The trackers may have figured out where you live. I am not sure.

Grand clutched the green memory-in-a-bottle to his chest like it was his only child.

As I said before, I have come to deliver this message to you from Huron. You're the steward of Huron. Only the steward has the power to protect the Merrows. The voice will guide him, the voice of Huron. I think the trackers want to stop you from returning home and saving them. We must shake those devilish creatures loose. If I don't bring you back to your place and time in history, the Merfolk shall perish. Start packing your bags, grandson. I have sworn to return you, Nikolas Lyons.

Please respond and let me know you're getting these messages.

Chapter Five
R-5235

uron...

...Steward...

...Nikolas...

...Rones...

...Peril of us all...

...Steward...

Ever since the fire marshal had escorted them to their bedrooms, the woman's words banged around Nick's head like a really bad jingle. Even now, he could feel Huron's cobblestone road under his boots and hear the crackle of the blue flames of that katana as it warmed his hand and face.

Presently, both Lyons brothers were lying on their beds. They were shimmering red, except where protective eyewear had been—an effect from the sudden burst of solar radiation from the Prometheus 10,000 just before it blew up. Tim lay sideways with his mouth slightly open. Nick kept a determined gaze on the plastic alloy ceiling.

From somewhere on the other side of the bed he heard the familiar whirling of anti-grav motors.

"That was quick," Nick said, without turning. "Hasn't even been a day."

"Good afternoon, Nick," the replacement nannydrone said. "It has been brought to my attention that you have been put on house arrest. Lucky it wasn't jail, you know."

"Mom and Dad have the fire marshal's bank account number. And *that's* how the world turns."

He rolled over, hoping the nannydrone would give up and go back to the corner where it could keep monitoring him in its creepy way. Instead, the anti-grav motors whirled as it rose above his left shoulder and leaned over.

"Nick?"

"Yeah?"

"Are you still attempting to run away, Nick?"

"Yes, if that's OK with you."

"Why?" Said the nannydrone.

"Why?" Nick waved his hands. "I've explained this, like, a million times to you. Oh right. You're a replacement. Well, I'm trying to get off this planet because people here are stupid. Entire world is covered with the Geneva virus. The earth hasn't seen the sun in years. All my friends are trapped in a refugee camp. And no one seems to care. They just worry about getting their next chin tuck. I'm tired of these people. I want out. Is that OK with you?"

"It is not my feelings on the subject you should be worried about, Nick," the nannydrone said. "It is your mother's. I have been collecting Sonya Lyons's social status messages regarding your attempts to run away. Would you like me to read them out to you, Nick?"

"Please don—"

"April 27th," the nannydrone ignored him. "At 3:14 pm, your mother wrote on her *Friendme* account." In a perfect mimic of her voice, the nannydrone quoted, "'What-ever. Caught Nick trying to break into my bank account last night. I was like crazy insomniac and found him creeping through my account, running one of those account-crack apps. Ugh!!! Where does he even get these programs? He was two clicks away from buying a shuttle ticket to outer space, AGAIN! Next time I'm gonna let him go. Anyone want a fourteen-year-old mentally disturbed demon-boy? Lol!!!!'"

"May 8th. 9:10 am."

"OK. You seriously cannot pay me enough to put up with demon-boy. Airport security arrested the boy for trying to hook up a leech pod to a Moonshuttle. Thought he could hitch a ride ON THE HULL OF A SPACE SHUTTLE!! Who does that? Seriously. Am I the only mom who puts up with this crap? #WishI-couldrunaway."

"June 2nd. 10:15 pm."

"Yep. Demon-boy almost lit Hiker's Canyon on fire. Of course. Oh, and he torched the neighbor's greenhouse. It is gone. GONE. Thank goodness for pyrodrones. Seriously."

"June 3rd. 1:23 am."

"Lighting Hiker's canyon on fire, remix. Again, pyrodrones put it out before we were sued by every person on the block. Found out he was messing around in the old tech shed. Blew something up. Probably trying to build a space shuttle. Seriously, that boy is the fuel of nightmares. #mysonisafuturemanhunt."

"My bio-rhythm sensors, which are sponsored by Pappy's Popsicles, tell me you are quite frustrated, and we just can't have that. What *you* need is a Pappy's Popsicle."

Nick fell back with a groan, thinking to himself, *What I need is to get off this planet.*

Probably should stop hearing voices in my head then. He frowned. *What did that woman say? The Rones lies about their true intent. They enter the city of Huron at the peril of us all.*

Nick supposed he should've been worrying about the failed invention or the fire marshal who threw out words like "Prozac" and "threat to all plant and animal life in a fifty-mile radius." Which wasn't fair, not really. Nick wasn't psychotic; he had never enjoyed torturing small animals. It was just that he was, well, optimistic. And sometimes that optimism led to the singing of a pine cone or two. Not that it really mattered. If you twisted your ankle, a dozen ambudrones would be right there. And if you accidentally set a tree on fire, pyrodrones would sweep in and have it out in minutes. Your every need and whim would be provided for you... well, *if* you were a "civil." On the other hand, if you had the unfortunate luck of being a refugee with a twisted ankle, BioFarms Corporation would lower your life expectancy by a year and send you a pamphlet directing you to make a cast out of old T-shirts and glue.

Seriously? Nick thought. *Tons of refugees die every day from lack of access to basic medicine when, just across the canyon, civils can receive a new heart as part of their outpatient surgery? What kind of a society does that?*

And by "society," Nick meant his parents.

When their grandfather, Nikolas Lyons the 11th, set up a trust fund with a never ending supply of money, his parents decided to take early retirement and move to one of Colorado City's suburbanhoods. His parents hadn't worked for five years now. Instead, they spent their days globe-shopping and burning through Grand's trust fund.

But Nick wouldn't get sucked in. *What did Grand always say?*

"You must arise, Nikolas, and take your place among the clouds."

Hospitality 3000 announced, "Sonya Lyons, identified. Heart rate: Excited. Condition: Healthy. Geneva infection levels: 0.00.

Erik Lyons, identified. Heart rate: Excited. Condition: Healthy. Geneva infection levels: 0.00.

Beep, beep.

House secure."

Nick heard the clop of boots. Fast voices echoed downstairs.

Beep, the intercom alerted.

"Nick and Tim!" Their mom shouted through the intercom. "Get your freaky pyromaniac rears down here now!"

A holographic image of an Asian news anchor in a three-piece tweed suit stood over the mantle. He thanked his co-host and began his segment. "Reports coming in from the villages of the African Federation to the most northern region of Alaska have confirmed that we are, indeed, experiencing the second greatest outbreak of the Geneva virus. There are 278,000 confirmed deaths reported throughout the Global Union. As of last May, more marriages have ended by the Geneva virus than divorce. The U.S. will open its 35th intranational refugee camp by month's end. A bill is currently in the International Council to replace refugee fences with walls, no longer allowing refugee minors to cross its bord—"

A computer voice cut off the broadcaster. "Forgive the interruption, but the bio-rhythm sensors indicate a hostile confrontation between Sonya and Erik Lyons and their two sons, Nick and Tim Lyons. Would you like me to record the teleholo for another time?"

"You bet," their mother said in her pitchy voice. She held two large shopping bags on each hand like the Lady of Justice. Her fingers flared, sending both bags to the ground.

"Oh. My. Gosh," She shoved her sunglasses into her hair, giving the impression of a blond peacock that had just gotten back from a shopping spree. "Like, seriously, Nick. This is so beyond irresponsible. Your son, Erik. *Your* son is mentally ill."

Nick looked slowly to his father. He'd just had the tips of his blond hair and soul patch re-highlighted. The stylist had gotten a little aggressive around his eyebrows and one was shorter than the other.

"Bro..." his father said, snapping his finger. A housedrone whizzed into the room holding two diet soda bottles. "Come on. I thought we were tight, bro."

In case someone was wondering, yes. Nick's mom and dad had the collective maturity of a thirteen-year-old.

"Erik and I were sitting there," their mom started while opening the diet sodas and passing one to their dad. "And I'm in the middle of a back skin regeneration, which can*not* be interrupted, and guess what? The fire marshal calls me. The fire marshal? Again? And they're telling me you've burned a forest down or something? Whatever, Nick. Seriously. What. Ever." She tipped her head back and downed half the bottle of diet soda.

"The pyrodrones were there in thirty seconds flat,"

Nick said. "The machine singed like ten trees and maybe an azalea. They'll inject it with growth therapy, and it'll be good as new. Probably already is."

Their dad smacked his lips after an equally deep guzzle from the soda and shook his flipped hair. "You two are crazy-town crazy."

"Hey. It's not my fault, Dad, er, bro-Dad." Tim said, pointing to Nick. "He's trying to build an invention to raise money. He's going to run away to Moon."

"We had a deal." Nick gritted his teeth.

"Yeah. We did," Tim snapped back. "And you broke that deal. I told you I didn't want help with Rocky. And—and he got into your stuff, too, Dad. Took your solar battery and memory chip."

"My stuff?" their dad said, completely ignoring the fact that he'd just learned his son was trying to run away. "What do you mean, my *stuff*?"

"He was in the garage—"

"Doing what?" His dad stood up.

Nick leaned into his brother. "Seriously, Tim. You do not know pain."

"He took apart your hover utility vehicle," Tim mumbled, wincing as Nick clenched his fist.

"He did WHAT-TA?" His dad's eyes grew. "I know you didn't touch my Validate, bro. I know you didn't. What did I say? What. Did. I. Say? I said to stay on your side of the garage. You don't see me messing with your stuff!" Their dad's sandals flapped quickly as he marched into the garage.

"It worked though," Nick called after him. "The solar battery worked. I stored the light in it and shot it out."

"I so don't care if it worked." Their mom followed. "Keep your freaky hands off Erik's stuff. It ain't yours. Wait until I tell your granddaddy."

"Whaaa..." Their dad's voice dried up. "WHAT DID YOU DO TO MY VALIDATE?!"

"Nick!" His mom screamed from the garage, and he heard the shattering of a diet soda bottle. "Your dad's H.U.V.! Are you insane?"

Nick had completely dismantled the engine.

"I—I needed the solar battery and motherboard," Nick said. "I've always put it back together."

"You did this before?" their mom said.

"One time—"

"Ten times," Tim corrected.

"I swear, Nick Lyons," their mom said, "you better put every wire and chip back in its place."

"Yeah. About that." Nick took a step back. "The experiment was a resounding success, but it sorta blew up the Validate's battery and—and the motherboard. This might be a good time to contact your insurance company."

Nick's dad kept attempting words, but none seemed to relate to the English language. He was beet red, and his mouth looked like it was trying to decide between screaming and crying.

Their mom spun on her heel and balled up her fists.

"What did I tell you would happen, Nick, if you got your hands on one more electronic device?"

Nick's eyes grew.

"I've had it with you, freak!" she screamed. "You're getting the inhibitors tonight."

"What?" Nick looked to his dad. Everything just turned really serious. Neural inhibitors were given to kids who were considered dangerous and out of control. Nick would be seventeen the next time he could string together an entire sentence.

Their mother pointed upstairs. "Get up to your rooms now! The doctor will transmit a prescription to your nannydrone."

The brothers marched slowly up to their rooms.

"Why don't you shut your mouth?" Nick said, just as their bedroom door slid closed. "I protected you from Rocky. You know what? Next time she can ape all over you for all I care."

"I told you I didn't want your help," Tim said. "Besides, you destroyed Dad's Validate. And for what? Another attempt at arsony? Sorry, dude, but electronics are the last thing you should touch."

"It was coming together," Nick sighed. "Almost had it ready. Would have won that money, too."

"You *almost* burned down a forest, Nick. Someone's got to stop you."

"If you want to make an omelette, you gotta crack a few eggs."

"Exactly!" Tim waved his hands. "You know who

said that, Nick? Stalin said that. Stalin—who committed genocide against his *own* people."

"Well—we don't know *who* really said that." Nick pounded the intercom. He had rewired it two-way so he could eavesdrop on his parents. It came in handy when planning a sneak out.

His dad's voice trembled. "My Validate! That crazy punk kid took apart my Validate!"

"I told him what I'd do," their mom said. "He's insane. He's just insane.... Yes?... Um. Yeah. I need that doctor—you know, the one who gives neural inhibitors. He's on the MediNetwork, right?... Yeah... No. We already have a file opened in the psychiatric wing.... Yes. We have a nannydrone.... Yeah, she better be able to process all forms of medication. We paid, like, a fortune for her."

"Whatever." Nick fell back on the bed, focusing his brow on some point in the ceiling. "It is time I leave this den of parental totalitarianism."

"Call the national guard," Tim said. "The monster is loose and headed for New York harbor."

"You seem distressed, Nick Lyons." The nannydrone crept toward him.

"Now is *not* the time," Nick said. "Planning my escape."

"Hmm. I wonder what might make you happy today. Perhaps—" The nannydrone lifted its right arm holding an unwrapped popsicle. "A complementary Pappy's popsicle?"

"I. Don't. Want. It!" Nick jumped to his feet. "I don't want a Pappy's Popsicle, or Pudding Fingers, or Dipping Sticks. And I don't want a digital head floating in my face, selling me junk all the time!" He grabbed the popsicle and threw it.

The nannydrone spun, shooting several laser beams to intercept the popsicle fragments before they hit the wall.

"That was a close one." The nannydrone grabbed the popsicle stick. "Cleanliness is next to happin— Please stand by for a transmission from St. Mary's MediNetwork.... I have received your mother's request to administer the neural inhibitor, R-5235." The popsicle-free hand flipped like a switchblade, revealing a long, silvery needle. The nannydrone moved slowly toward Nick.

"Crap." Nick sat straight up.

"Dude," Tim said. "Mom didn't waste any time."

"Nothing to be concerned about," the nannydrone said. "This medication is not fatal. It will simply suppress any and all aggressive thoughts and behaviors. Common side effects may include dizziness, memory loss, aversion to social environments, difficulty with complex verbal communication and thinning of the hair. It is a very efficient medication, if I do say so myself. One shot will last up to thirty-six months or three years."

The nannydrone spun around with the popsicle stick in its other hand and headed toward the trash compactor. "But my primary protocol is to clean up your mess first. Afterward, I will administer the drug."

Nick stood to his feet.

The trash compactor slid open.

Nick raised his right tennis shoe.

The nannydrone raised the popsicle stick over the compactor.

Nick kicked. Before the nannydrone could escape the compactor, he slammed the door.

Muffled commands came from the trash compactor. "Open the compartment, Nick Lyons. The nannydrone is in severe danger of being destroye—"

Nick tapped the button: *COMPACT.*

The compactor moaned as it tried to crush the nannydrone.

"Please open the compartment," the nannydrone repeated. "The nannydrone is in severe danger of b—eing damaged or—d—estro—Would you lik—executable file—chocoberry—R-5235—yum three-hundred and Pappy'sssssssssssszzz—"

The compactor moaned one last time before accepting its victim.

"You scare me," Tim said.

"A nannydrone just tried to turn my brains to mush, and I scare you?"

An explosion of glass came from downstairs. Both boys turned to the intercom.

"Erik? Erik! What's wrong?" their mom cried.

The door swished, and Nick flew down the stairs.

"Dad?"

His dad lay in a halo of glass, still gripping the bottle of diet soda. He was lathered in sweat and blood. From what Nick could tell, he had collapsed onto their coffee table.

"Dad!" Tim yelled. "Is it the Geneva virus?"

Nick's mom tapped her ear and shouted, "9-1-1!"

The earpiece answered, "Dialing..."

An electronic voice answered, "9-1-1. What is your emergency?"

Nick's mom sobbed into the phone, "Erik—Erik! Something's wrong with Erik!"

Sweat ran down their dad's puffy red face. Tim tried to prop him up.

"Don't touch him!" screamed their mom. "Yes? No, I was talking to Tim.... OK. I won't hang up."

Within sixty seconds, a hoverbulance's siren descended to the front of the house. A woman with a black bag and an ambudrone met Nick at the door.

"He's over there." Nick turned to his dad. Blood had now moved past the glass and onto the Persian rug.

Hospitality 3000 announced, "Ambulance attendant Cheryl Sierra has now entered. Condition: Healthy. Heart rate: Normal. Geneva infection levels: 0.00. Ambudrone has now entered. Condition: Unavailable. Heart rate: Unavailable.

Beep, beep.

House secure."

The attendant opened her black bag and pressed a

small thin square on their dad's chest. She fiddled with an earpiece, paused, and pursed her lips.

"What?" Nick looked at her.

The attendant quickly placed a square piece on Nick's chest. Cold metal pressed through his shirt. She repeated it with Tim, then their mom. The attendant paused, looked at the diet soda in their father's hand, and closed her bag.

"Was it the diet sodas?" their mom said.

"Ma'am," The attendant didn't answer her. "We need to get you and your husband to the ER, now!"

Their mom croaked through tears, "Wha—?"

"Please, ma'am, follow us." The attendant turned to the boys. "Next of kin?"

"Our Grandpa, Grand," Nick answered. "Nikolas Lyons, the 11th."

"Call him now. Meet us at St. Mary's ER."

Another ambulance attendant came in with a stretcher. It was a whirlwind of limbs and lifting and dispatches to the ER.

Hospitality 3000 announced, "Ambulance attendant Cheryl Sierra has now left the premises. Heart rate: Excited. Condition: Healthy. Geneva infection levels: 0.00.

Ambulance attendant Robert Killigan has now left the premises. Heart rate: Excited. Condition: Healthy. Geneva infection levels: 0.00.

An ambudrone has now left the premises.

Erik Lyons has now left the premises. Heart rate: Low. Condition: Critical. Geneva infection levels: 0.00.

Sonya Lyons has now left the premises. Heart rate: Excited. Condition: Critical. Geneva infection levels: 0.00.

Timothy Lyons has now left the premises. Heart rate: Excited. Condition: Healthy. Geneva infection levels: 0.00."

This is Grand again.

The inside of Grand's hovertruck rattled under the blows of a summer storm. He gripped the wheel, his eyes fixed on Nick's videomail message camera.

The digital readout read:

CALLER: GRAND LYONS (GRANDPA)
TIME 8:52 PM
LOCATION: COLORADO CITY, COLORA-DO

I fear you haven't been getting my messages about Machu Picchu and the Merfolk. That I have a message for you in this bottle!

Grand shoved the memory-in-a-bottle into the viewscreen. A lightning flashed and the screen shook. He screamed, *Blasted!* as the bottle rolled out of his hands and into the passenger seat. He tried to hold onto the steering while searching for the bottle.

There you go. He pulled the bottle to his chest. *I am twenty minutes away. I must warn you. There are devilish creatures on my tail. Trackers. Scuccas to be exact. They have hunted me for years. It's why I have never left my truck. I mean to protect you and Tim from them. Nevertheless, be careful. If you see anything suspicious, if someone becomes suddenly ill or poisoned, know it is the trackers. They have found you. It isn't me they've been hunting. It is you, Nikolas Lyons.*

Hope to hear from you soon.

Kevin Rayfield McGill

Chapter Six
St. Mary's

"Lyons. My name is Nick Lyons," Nick answered the St. Mary's nursedrone sitting behind the front desk.

"Full name, please," the nursedrone said, tilting her plastic alloy head to emulate a person asking a question.

"That's my full name. Grand calls me Nikolas, and so does Caroline Wendell, I guess, but Nick is the name on the birth certificate."

"How may I help you?" the nursedrone said.

"My mom and dad were drinking diet sodas, and they got really, I don't know, sick, or poisoned, or—"

"ErikandSonyaLyons!" Tim had just caught up.

"Your parents are in the Disease and Poison Emergency Wing." The nursedrone pressed a button. "A Nick and Tim Lyons are here for Erik and Sonya Lyons."

A female voice from the console answered, "Send them to the waiting room. I've a few questions about their parents' files. Their biochemistry is off the charts..." The voice walked away.

The nursedrone pointed down the hall. "Follow the signs to the Disease and Poison Emergency Waiting Room."

They took off running. The white plastic walls reflected their desperate sprint.

Zzzzzz.

A small white sphere with green scanning eyes floated next to them. It was an inocudrone.

"MediOne records tell me—" The inocudrone paced with them. "—that Nick Lyons and Tim Lyons have not received their inoculation shots for fifteen days. Remember that forty new strands of the cold and five new mutations of the Geneva virus have appeared in only the last forty-eight hours. Please remain still as I administer the vaccine."

Tim and Nick stopped and obediently put their arms out to the inocudrone. There are two places on the planet you never want to be without your inoculations: the refugee camps and the hospital.

The inocudrone was cycling through its third and last shot when Nick heard a voice come from around the corner.

"Receiving a new transmission from MediOne, Nick," came a motherly digital voice. It was a nanny-drone.

"Another replacement?!" Nick said, turning on his heels.

The nannydrone sped up with the needle pointed at him. "You are to receive the neural inhibitor, R-5235, Nick."

Nick jumped back and barely missed the lance.

"R-5235 is designed to suppress all aggression, Nick." The nannydrone aimed its needle at Nick's stomach and thrust again.

Nick sidestepped quickly, looked to the two in-ocudrones, and commanded. "Inocudrones. The nan-nydrone has been contaminated with, uh, the black plague! You have to stop it from spreading."

The inocudrones immediately swiveled to the nan-nydrone and replaced their needles with blasters. "Must eliminate all biological threats!" The inocudrones said in unison. "Must eliminate all biological threats!"

The nannydrone turned, flipping its needle with its own blaster, but it was too late. The inocudrones fired. Red bursts of light smashed the nannydrone to the wall. The sound of blasters reverberated through-out the hallway causing nearby drones to pivot in their direction.

"Come on." Nick tore into another run.

Tim tried to keep up with his brother. "What just

happened?"

They charged through the sliding doors into a packed waiting room divided into refugees and suburbanites. One side wore tattered, mismatched clothes, while the other wore that week's hottest fashion. Although their clothes were different, their expressions remained the same: fear.

Among the suburbanites was a mother wearing a *Robin's Little League* T-shirt and matching hat and holding her three-year-old daughter. The mother covered her mouth, crying bitterly as a doctor spoke under hushed breath. Nick couldn't hear what the doctor was saying, but he could guess. The mother and child left with the doctor, opening up two seats for the brothers.

"What's happening?" Tim said, as he plopped down next to an old, snoring hover-bus driver.

"I don't know," Nick shrugged.

"So, if it's not the Geneva virus, what is it?" Tim said.

"I don't know."

"Where's Grand?" Tim said.

Nick sighed, "I don't know." He wondered why their grandfather hadn't called them for almost a month, which reminded him. The EMT ordered him to call his nearest kin. He flipped over his wrist and turned on the wrist-phone.

You have six new messages from your grandpa, the phone announced.

"Woah!" Nick sat up. "Grand's been trying to get

ahold of us."

"What?" Tim leaned over.

"That's crazy. Where is he going?"

Last Nick heard their grandfather was a project leader at some archaeological dig in Machu Picchu. He held the wrist phone up to Tim and scrolled through the videomail's times and locations.

"Look at this. He's been everywhere."

LOCATION: MACHU PICCHU
LOCATION: SANTORINI, GREECE
LOCATION: BEIJING, CHINA
LOCATION: COLORADO CITY, COLORA-
DO

"Colorado City... ?" Nick's head shot up. "Tim. Grand is here! He's in Colorado C—!"

"My grandsons!" A thick, foreign accent came from the other side of the doors. "Where are they?"

"Please, Mr. Lyons," said an inocudrone in a cautionary tone. "You cannot go any farther until I take a reading."

Nick looked at the doors.

"I am collecting some very disturbing vitals," the inocudrone said.

"My grandsons!" the voice bellowed.

Everyone's gaze shifted to the man on the other side of the emergency room doors.

"Mr. Lyons!" the inocudrone said. "Not only are you 6020 days overdue for your inoculation shots, I am detecting fifteen viruses, one of them predating the

Iron Age, twelve forms of bacteria found only on the south side of Moon, and a form of metal that cannot be found on the periodic table whatsoever. I am processing the necessary vaccines now. Wait one moment, please."

"I would be pleased, hubcap," the foreign-sounding voice said, "if you took three paces in the opposite direction."

"I will need to administer thirteen different vaccines," the inocudrone announced. "Five through the arm. Seven through the nose. And one—"

FRZEEESHHHH! came the sound of an exploding inocudrone.

"Grand!" the brothers said, jumping to their feet.

The door slid open revealing a shower of sparks and a swarthy looking man. Their grandfather, Grand, with his white and yellow marbled beard stood like some Viking out of time. He wore a green trench coat plastered in dirt. After three great steps, he pulled the brothers into a hug that smelled of sweat and hovertruck. Nick returned the hug. Tim stiffened.

"My boys!" Grand said.

"Wait a second," Tim raised his hands. "You never come down here. I thought an 'evil shadow' covered the face of Earth or something?"

"Nikolas!" Grand grabbed Nick by the shoulder and pulled out an antique green bottle. He started waving it in Nikolas's face. "Have you gotten any of my messages? That I finally cracked Ludwig's puzzle? That the

Merrows are under attack and Huron needs you?!"

"Huron—How do you know about the voice?" Nick said. "And is it on Moon?"

"Well." Grand's head tilted. "Yes. It is Moon. Not the Moon you know. And you don't really call it Moon... "

Nick hated to tell Grand he was babbling again. His grandfather was his most favorite person in the world, but he had a tendency to scatter-talk. You just had to go along for the ride.

"Moon?" Tim said. "Wait. What's a Merrow?"

"Mermen," Grand said. "You know. Fishpeople. They've been attacked by Dujinnin, and they call for Nikolas's aid. I have to take you into the past to save them—the Merfolk on the Moon, that is."

Nick could only stare back at him. He knew Grand had been a little loony, but did he just utter the word Merfolk?

As if Grand understood his confusion, he patted his dirty trench coat, mumbling something. "Where is it? There's a better way to explain this to you.... Ah, there you go." He pulled out a small vial, unscrewed a tin lid, poured something out into his hand and held it up.

"Ugh," Tim leaned in. "That's a bug, Grand. And it's dead."

In their grandfather's hand lay a dead fly. Its feet were curled and sticking up.

"Right." Nick frowned. "What exa—"

Before he could finish his sentence, Grand grabbed his hand and dropped the fly into it. Nick flinched, a little grossed out by the idea of touching some deceased bug. But when he opened his hand, he realized it was actually a tiny mechanical robot. It looked to be made out of tin, constructed with tiny gears and rivets.

"It's a wallfly," Grand said, "invented by one of my good friends, Ludwig the Toymaker. The device does exactly what you think. It covertly follows individuals, recording what they see. They came in quite handy during the Kraken revolt of '24." Grand pointed to the fly. "Go on, Nikolas. Watch the recording."

"Wha—how?" Nick said.

"With the memory-in-a-bottle, of course.... Oh, right. Haven't given that to you yet." Remembering he had the green memory-in-a-bottle in his clutches, Grand held it to Nick. He wondered where his grandfather would've even found a bottle like that. There were only a few of them left in the Smithsonian.

He took it. The glass felt greasy, probably from his grandfather's dirt-covered palms.

"OK," Grand motioned. "Put the mouth to your eye. Look inside the bottle."

"Sure," Nick shrugged. He lifted the bottle's mouth to his eyeball and looked inside.

"It's just the inside of a bottle," Nick said. It's not as if he'd expected something different.

"No, no. Put the wallfly *inside* the bottle," Grand pointed.

Nick nodded and dropped the wallfly into the bottle. It clanked and then began to shake.

The bottle flashed bright blue.

"Woah!" Nick almost dropped it.

After the flash, the inside of the bottle changed. He could now make out what appeared to be a tiny replica of a dark sea smashing up against a white cliff face. On the cliff, a man was driving two small stagecoaches.

"The wallfly's memory has been deposited into the memory-in-a-bottle," Grand said. "*Now* put the bottle to your eye."

"Um, OK." Nick closed his right eye and slowly lifted the small mouth of the bottle to his left one. The second it sealed around his eyeball he found himself floating over a cliff-face. The smell of saltwater filled his nose, and he winced at a bitter cold wind.

"That's crazy!" Nick pulled the bottle away, stumbling backward. One moment he had been in a hospital, and the next he was floating over an ocean.

"Where is this from, Grand?" He finally said, holding up the bottle. "Is it some advanced virtual reality system?"

"No." Grand stomped his foot. "That's from Möon. Your home."

Nick slowly lifted it, squinting his cheeks as he tried to peer through the green glass.

He remembered bottles like these from the last time they had visited the Smithsonian; "ship-in-a-bottle" is what the tour guide called them. Several of them were filled with miniature sea ships, but others were filled with miniature mansions, farmhouses, even a few rocket ships. The tour guide said that the craftsman would meticulously construct the miniatures inside the bottle with long-handled tools, basically rebuilding the ship inside with teeny-tiny tweezers. But the tour guide never said the bottles were, in fact, memory projectors from the Moon.

"It's an elven creation—the bottle," their grandfather explained. "It may feel real, but it is nothing more than the memories of a person or creature. You can drop a hair follicle, chip of a tooth, even a piece of clothing into it. The memory-in-a-bottle will recreate the object's memory. Having put the wallfly inside the bottle, you will relive what it experienced. You should know you can re-experience the wallfly's journey, but you cannot change the events."

"Sure," Nick said nervously. Slowly this time, he placed his eye onto the bottle's opening. Instantly he found himself flying toward the stagecoaches. The fog and rain beat at his face, making him squint. Since he was, in part, reliving the wallfly's experience, his flight path was loopy and not the most direct, but eventually, he made it to the driver. Just before he rose eye-level to the driver, Nick saw his reflection in the stagecoach window with the aid of the lamplights. Staring back at him was the mechanical fly. Its tiny red ruby eyes inspected the window for a moment.

The wallfly rose until it was next to the driver. The man wore a tricorn hat, long frock coat, and knee britches. Nick was impressed by the man's costume. He looked like he'd just stepped out of the American Revolution or one of those games with British redcoats and pirates with their long muskets.

Nick looked back to Grand again but had to give himself a minute to say anything because the room was still spinning.

"Grand... this can't be Moon," He said slowly. "It is a desolate rock. There are no mermen on the Moon or at all!"

Grand's lip started to curl. "No. There are none *now*, but there used to be, when this was recorded to be exact. And its name isn't Moon. It's Möon."

"Möon?" Nick turned his head.

"Yes, Nikolas. Möon."

"Ok, fine." Nick decided to drop that crazy line of conversation. "Who is the man driving the stagecoach?"

"It is Yeri Willrow. The wallfly followed him through a dangerous journey as he escorted a group of Merfolk to their fortress back on Möon. I've watched it half a dozen times. I would suggest you experience it for yourself. Only then will you understand the grave danger the Merfolk are in and why they need you.

"OK," Nick said flatly. What else could he say? He looked at the memory-in-a-bottle and then put it back to his eye for the third time.

In the form of the wallfly, he swept around the stagecoach until he was eye-to-eye with the driver, Yeri Willrow. At that moment the stagecoach driver looked back and shrieked. Nick could see hundreds of red eyes and the teeth of a piranha running toward them.

The driver bellowed, "Möon down my boots!"

.

A long time ago in a world
not so far away...

World of Möon
Eynclaene Province,
Gromwell Village

Chapter Seven
Foggy Flight

öon down my boots!" Yeri swore, well, judging by his mother's standards.

The stagecoach wheel had nearly slipped, threatening to throw driver and passengers to the frothing sea below. Yes, Yeri took the stagecoach driver's oath to "guide passengers through every hazard and peril." Still, he didn't have to enjoy it, especially when a devilish creature with red-pronged eyes gave chase all the way from Gromwell village on one of the foggiest nights of his illustrious stagecoach driving career. When the fog had thickened so that Yeri couldn't see its red eyes or his own nobbly hands for that matter, he could rely on the smell. The monster reeked of rotten onion.

He looked up in time to see a black shape envelop him and screamed, "Aaah!"

He opened his eyes and patted his frock coat. No teeth ripping flesh from body. No blood being dispensed from its human vessel.

"Just a misty mirage, ol' boy," Yeri chuckled to himself.

Grauhh! came a soul-curdling roar. The horses jerked away from the noise.

Nick, now experiencing all of this in the form of the wallfly, jumped at the sound of the monster. He knew this was just some kind of memory device invented by Grand's friend, Ludwig, but that sounded VERY real. He wondered if he was about to see this man, Yeri, be torn up by some freaky mutant creature.

"That was no mirage," Yeri said, trying to steady the horses. But their nerves got the best of them, and they darted left, forcing the stagecoach wheels to skate across the cliff face again. Just when he thought they would descend to their briny death, wheels grabbed rock, and the stagecoach righted itself. Yeri was one of the more able drivers, but if they did not reach their destination soon, either cliff or creature would win this race.

Of course, he was sufficiently capable of driving the horses above a scamper, if it wasn't for the double stagecoach. Mr. Fungman was always trying to save a sulmare and so devised the two-hitched stagecoach, allowing him to charge twice as much for every driver. Well,

Mr. Fungman didn't have to steer these monstrosities around every sheer drop.

A pounding fist came from inside the coach. Yeri thought to ignore the passenger's need, but that was another oath he had taken.

Maybe he should stop taking so many oaths.

Yeri pulled the reigns, and the horses whinnied to a stop. He scrambled from the stagecoach, pulled out a key, and grasped the iron latch. Then he changed his mind.

"Please, sir," Yeri tried to control his gasps. "For, uhm—er—your safety, it's best we continue."

"Let me out, driver."

Yeri's eyes darted from door to highway to door. Come to think of it, he hadn't met the passengers, being charged with them at the very last moment. The previous driver had come down with squatters. Jameson's face was covered in budding, orange flowers.

The key spun past tumblers, and Yeri swung the door open. Lamplights washed away any view of the passengers, but what he couldn't see, he could hear. There were gears on gears turning and belts locking into place. Slowly, something that looked like a collection of spokes and cranks crafted by a mad clockmaker emerged from the coach. The gears turned out to be legs—automaton legs, an invention and wonder used only by the wealthy.

The man must be a cripple, he thought.

Leather gloves reached out to the edges of the door,

and the man pulled himself out.

Yeri gasped.

The passenger didn't have two gnarled legs, but one long, iridescent fishtail. It bent where knees should bend with a wide fin and a line of sharp, bony protrusions outlining the dorsal. The automalegs seemed to be a near extension of the man's upper body.

"Thank you, driver," the passenger said. "Unable to hear over the horses."

"Dear me. Ve—very sorry sir." Yeri removed his hat. "Jameson was sick, and I was unaware, of—er—your handicap, sir. I took zoology, of course, but it was only for extra credit, and my teacher was a blunderbuss of the highest ord—"

"Do not concern yourself, driver. It is no handicap. Now please, silence."

"Forgive me, sir. One should be of more assistance, Mister... ?" Yeri said with eyes locked on the passenger's fishtail.

"Lir," the merman sighed. Evidently, Yeri's curiosity was greater than Lir's need for silence. "My name is Lir Anu Palus, and this is Nia Menweir Palus. We are the Duke and Duchess of the Eynclaene Coastlands."

The woman he called Nia pushed her head out and offered a smile.

"Duke and Duchess?" Yeri's mouth widened and then he quickly bowed. "I am Yeri Willrow, senior stagecoach driver for Fungman, Zedock, and Josiah Stagecoach Company. And at your utmost service."

Even with the fog's white plumes rolling past, Yeri could see that Lir was strong, with commanding features and bluish-gray eyes. He was wearing gentlemen's leather gloves and a red silk frock. Oddly enough, though his hair was deep silver, he had the features of a young man. Yet Nia was the one who captured the gaze of the stagecoach driver. She had a quiet, slender frame and the kind of crystal eyes that would liquefy the heart of any man.

Yeri had no doubt that they were a duke and a duchess, for both were garnished with jewelry more valuable than the whole of Gromwell village. Yeri felt his own stark contrast. He was orphan-thin except for a gourd-shaped midsection, a nose like an elbow, and lips that couldn't fully close. More so, his wilting hat and tattered knee-breeches didn't speak of a man who would come into his fortune anytime soon.

"Is—Is it painful?" Yeri said. "Not being near water and all?"

"I have not lost my humling nature," Lir laughed.

"Please understand, sir." Yeri took off his hat. "I have never set my eyes upon a mermaid, aside from a few schoolbooks."

"Yes, indeed," Lir said, "which explains your lack of anatomical observation."

"Sir?" Yeri wrinkled his brow.

"I am no maid. I am a merman. But anyway, we are called Merrows."

"Merrows." Yeri mouthed the word. His eyes darted

to the second coach. "The passengers—in there. They're Merrows, too?"

"Yes," Lir said, glancing back at the stagecoach. "My brother and sister-in-law. We were taking a well-needed rest after months of patrolling the coast of Eynclaene. Now, afraid I'll still need that moment of silence."

Lir raised his ear to the fog. Slowly, he sidestepped to the coach, opened the door, and retrieved what Yeri could only describe as a small harpoon attached to a handheld catapult.

Yeri turned his own ear to the night sky. "Can't hear them coming before the devils are upon you. Quiet as anything and fast as death, you know."

Lir held his hand up, signaling silence. "I am able to hear a sea urchin sneeze forty knots out to sea if I wish."

"Are they after the horses you suppose," Yeri said, "or are they hungry for man flesh?"

"No," Lir said, "they pursue me and my kin."

"You?" Yeri said. "Why you?"

Lir shook his head. "The answer to that would change the course of your life forever, driver. Afraid I cannot tell you.... Oh, and you are correct. They are fast."

"Pardon me?" Yeri said.

Lir's automalegs spun him around. "To the horses, now!"

Yeri, bug-eyed, grabbed the rail. He pulled himself up, buttocks last. With a bit of squirming, he found himself up right.

"Lift me up." Lir held a hand out.

Yeri hooked his foot to the railing and reached over. With a grunt, Yeri heaved the merman onto the passenger seat. The automalegs slipped off Lir and clattered to the ground.

"Get going, you lame muck snipes!" Yeri cracked the whip like a runaway windmill. The horses kicked dirt and leapt into a gallop. As a rule, he didn't like to yell at his horses, but now was not the time for rules.

Something shook the rear of the second stagecoach. Yeri turned to see claws shoved into wood, slowing the coaches down. The merman raised his harpoon and whispered something. The harpoon blazed with fire just as it sprung from the catapult.

Raiiggh! The creature lit into a ball of flames and tumbled into the mist.

He retrieved the harpoon by a thin cord. Several more cries came from everywhere, from nowhere.

"There are more?" Yeri said.

"Do you have anything useful?" Lir's voice competed with the grinding wheels. "A charm or maybe jynn'us?"

"No charms, sir, and no useful weapons..." Yeri's voice trailed off.

"Jynn'us?" Lir said. "Do you have jynn'us?!"

"Well, I—I can make toys come to life," Yeri offered, "which would explain Mum's ban on any and all toys since the age of eight. Lonely years, as you can imagine. I do wonder if things would've turned out different for me and Agatha if Mum had afforded me but a few toys."

"Thank you, Yeri." Lir pounded the roof.

Nia tried her best to lean out the window.

"The door prize," Lir said.

"It was for Mother," Nia contended.

"We are two breaths from death, dear," Lir shouted. "Might we save our domestic disputes for some less life-threatening circumstance?"

Nia disappeared and then leaned out, holding a tin box with an 'L' painted on top. "Here. Do be careful!"

"There you go, Yeri." Lir shoved the box into Yeri's hand. "That's a Ludwig. No better display of toymanship."

"A Ludwig—the famous toymaker? And this is his?" Yeri licked his chops as he slid the top open. "I've always wanted a Ludwig."

"It's a Roc. Very good," Lir said.

Yeri's left eye quivered. "Oh, sir. There must be a better way to rid ourselves of these monsters. It's a Ludwig, for Pete's sa—"

"Yeri," Lir warned.

"Really, sir, Rocs are a beast of burden. It would be cruel to send such a creature into the grips of batt—"

"Yeri!"

"Very well." Yeri resolved himself. He gently unwrapped the toy from its velvet bed. It looked like a horned eagle with tattered wings, and its neck was featherless.

"Simply brilliant," Yeri mourned. He covered the toy with his right hand. Smoky, bluish light sifted between his fingers.

"Ouiwww!" Yeri howled and pulled his hand back. With a leap, the Roc hovered eye level before its audience. "Little troglodyte bit me!"

"Yeri. Aren't they a mite bigger?" Lir said.

"I said I could make a toy come alive, not change its size," Yeri said.

The finger-sized Roc turned its head toward the red-eyed assailants and roared. It leapt into the foggy wall.

Silence.

Aiihh! The foggy monster cried.

Raaishhh! The Roc responded.

Combative cries rang down the cliffside.

Lir held out a hand. "The whip, good man. The horses know what to do."

Without a word, he pushed the whip into Lir's hands. The merman held out the whip in his left, the fiery harpoon gun in his right, and closed his eyes.

"I could throw a shoe at it."

"Shh. I cannot hear them if you are spea—"

The whip shot across Yeri's nose.

Greeow! A cry came from the mist. Lir reeled in a black mass with hundreds of red eyes. The harpoon tore through its stomach, and the creature burst into filthy smoke as it tumbled over the cliff, leaving an acrid smell in its wake.

"What are they, sir?" Yeri said. The monster had been

so close he could have hugged it, yet the fog hid its shape.

Lir looked ready to speak, but his mouth stayed shut.

Hundreds of red eyes appeared before them. Lir cocked the whip. Suddenly, another creature grabbed the whip from behind, and Lir was dragged to the back of the coach. At the last moment, he anchored himself into an exposed ribbing.

"Gaah!" Lir cried. His tail was being shredded by the stony ground.

With the whip still in his hand, the merman's muscles exploded from neck to shoulder as he flung the creature ahead of the stagecoach. Monstrous screams were cut short by the trunk of a spruce tree.

Lir righted himself on the seat and pointed to an outcropping. "Just beyond Constance Cove, that's our destination."

"Lesterton's Point, sir? But—"

"Trust me, Yeri."

The horses swung right and seaward.

Nick, as the wallfly, tumbled in the air for a moment, trying to keep up with the horses' sudden turn. It corrected itself just as he heard Yeri yell to Lir.

"Sir! There is nothing here but ocean below."

"Ride hard, sir."

"But the cliff?"

"Do not stop!"

The stagecoach leapt into the gut of mist, leaving the cliff behind. The horses' forelegs reached out for ground, for hope.

Chapter Eight
Second Stagecoach

T he stagecoach leapt off the ground and toward the misty ocean. The mad merman had steered them over the cliff, and now all Yeri could do was wait for death at the jagged rocks below.

Nick sucked in air, wondering if the wallfly would follow them to the depths of the sea. He had to remind himself, again, that this was all a memory.

Suddenly a white archway sprung from the mist and stagecoach wheels slammed cobblestone. They blew past a gate. Then Yeri saw a second gate with something near heaven on the other side of it. Before he could decide whether they had, in fact, died and gone there, the stagecoach burst through a hall.

"Lower the gates. Both of them!" Lir commanded.

Metal scrapped and slammed. Yeri grabbed the reins until his knuckles ground together. The horses veered to a stop, panting out their run.

"Where am I?" Yeri asked, as he stumbled from the stagecoach.

"The Duke of Eynclaene's fortress," Lir said, "my home. One part fortress, one part submarine. We travel the seas, moving and submerging along the coastline at various points. It's quite possible you've never seen it docked at this port."

"It is quite possible," Yeri muttered to himself.

A guard fitted with automalegs approached the stagecoach. He bowed and said, "Your grace?"

"See about my brother and his wife." Lir pointed to the second stagecoach. "We'll each need a velle. And fetch Captain Jonn immediately."

Four ornate chairs on spindly wheels were being pushed toward them, which Yeri took to be the velles.

He looked around the fortress hall only to find several Merrows looking back at him, their expressions moving between various stages of amazement and bewilderment. Most were sitting in their own velles, some were in automalegs, and the rest were treading water in small pools. Even with all the curious forms of transportation, the stagecoach driver couldn't imagine how they moved from floor to floor without some kind of stairwell. Then he saw large silicon tubes filled with water and dark, Merrow shapes swimming through them. These tubes were all around—like translucent roots creeping here and there. Some disappeared into the ceiling, others in the small pools, while the rest threaded between walls and floor. The fortress itself looked entirely made from silicon and were traced with mollusks, snail shells, and the bones of other strange ocean creatures. The only metal structures were golden braces that secured the wall joints and edges. Yeri also noticed the sound of constant water drips, as if the fortress had been recently submerged and was shedding its ocean water.

"Oh, dear Nia," a voice snapped Yeri from his observations. "Child, child, child. Gallivanting about with the local commoners and in your condition?" The voice came from an elderly mermaid who was being pushed in a velle by her attendant. She wore a large, powdered wig, had a fake mole just above the right side of her lip, and was covered in makeup bordering on clownish. Maybe Yeri was being unfair; he never went for the more garish fashions.

"Had quite the ride, Mother," Nia said as her shaky hand gripped her chair. She lifted herself to the seat, her fin slipping into a small catch. "You would've been proud of our driver, Yeri Willrow."

"Yeri." Nia held a hand out. "My mother, Hydan. Mother, Yeri Willrow, our hero of the evening."

Hydan's wheelchair squared to Yeri. He was surprised to find himself looking eye-to-eye with the elderly mermaid. The velle was designed like a small tower so that no Merrow could be looked down on.

Yeri nodded. "My lady."

Hydan smiled back like a dog that had just learned to fetch. "Humling. We are very grateful." She pointed her chin back to Nia. "Though I cannot believe Lir would condone such a silly excursion, against my advisement, nonetheless. What with your headaches, dear child."

Lir's wheels spun him around. "Forgive my lapse of judgment. It seems I have *again* forgotten my humble position as Duke of all Eynclaene coastlands to the detriment of your esteemed position as mother-in-law, nagger of all things great and small."

Hydan's eyes shrunk icily. "You know Nia's headaches can leave her bed-ridden. How dare you make me out a malagrug for loving my only chil—?"

Nia breathed heavily. "Please, Mother, do not be upset. It was my idea. I refused to stay bound to the fortress another moment."

"Nevertheless, Nia," Hydan said, refusing to address Lir again. "You should head straight to your chambers."

"Lir needs me," Nia said. "We were attacked, again."

"Your grace," said a merman in armored automalegs. He had a square face, an assortment of earrings, and his hair was shaved on the sides. Yeri didn't know if Merrows had warriors, but this man would be a candidate. "Forgive me. I was being debriefed by our scouts."

"Captain Jonn," Lir said. "We must make way for

northern Eynclaene at submersion level. Alert any other Merrows to evacuate the Eynclaene coast and stay to their fortresses. We were assaulted by no less than four fouls down the—"

"Fouls, sir?" Captain Jonn said.

"Yes, yes. We must undock and move this fortress immediate—"

"That will be entirely impossible, sir," Captain Jonn said. "My scout bore witness to a fleet of ships bearing the Dujinnin's crimson flag along the coast line, sir."

"The Dujinnin?" Lir's eyes widened.

"Yes, sir. I'm afraid so, sir," Captain Jonn said. "Their waterdragons make fo—"

"Waterdragons?" Yeri shouted. "Here? But this is the eastern seas?"

Captain Jonn looked quickly at Yeri, sizing him up. "And a winged foul was seen among the crew, sir. They're hemming us in," Captain Jonn said. "What are your orde—"

A mermaid screamed.

Yeri spun around just as all the Merrows ran to the edges of the room and away from the second stagecoach.

"No!" Nia screamed and leapt from her mother's arms. "Oh, no!"

Two guards grabbed her by the shoulders as she tried to fling herself at the second stagecoach. Instead of Lir's brother and sister-in-law adjusting themselves into velles, a gelatinous substance shrouded in Merrow clothing lay in clumps between two wheels. The substance looked like skin, devoid of all its innards.

"Dear Möon!" Lir walked slowly past Nia.

"The monster breathed on your brother and sister-in-law," Captain Jonn said. "They've been turned, sir."

A second round of screams came from just behind the stagecoach as a merman was pulled underneath by what looked like two long tendrils. The crowd of Merrows broke into a panic.

"We've been breached, sir!" Captain Jonn looked to Lir. "The fouls are inside!"

"What is that?" Yeri said, trying to see over the swelling crowd.

"A pair of fouls are inside. Seal the hall!" Captain Jonn said to his guards. "Close the merways." The captain suddenly grabbed Yeri by the shoulder. "You cannot see this, driver."

Yeri tried to move toward the second stagecoach to get a glimpse of the monster, but Captain Jonn spun him away by the shoulder and dragged him alongside of Lir as they fled from whatever was loose in the hall.

Nick hoped the wallfly could get a better view of the monster than Yeri, but the fly had to dodge fleeing Merrows. After a moment, it found itself back at Yeri's side.

"Brother," Lir said quietly, while holding a sobbing Nia.

"The Dujinnin mean to trap all the Merrows along the coast..." Lir's voice trailed off for a moment as he looked back to the gelatinous glob and then snapped to attention. "They mean to trap us in here and turn us into—"

Something like the crashing of metal came from under the deck, and the fortress shuttered violently. A velle slammed into Yeri's thigh, as Merrows were flung from their automalegs and wheelchairs.

"To your battle station, Captain, and alert the fortress fleet," Lir ordered Captain Jonn as he tried to climb back into his velle. Do not delay, Captain Jonn. Our very lives might come down to minutes. And see if we can get word to the steward."

"Excuse me?" Captain Jonn said.

"We need the Steward of Huron," Lir said, buckling himself into his automalegs. "He is our only hope. We need Nikolas Lyons."

Kevin Rayfield McGill

Chapter Nine
Waterdragons &
Obmorcrabs

"L yons?" Captain Jonn said. "Steward Nikolas Lyons? But, sir, he was taken away as a child. Lost from time and space."

"We'll need to find him then," Lir said.

"Very well," Captain Jonn said, turning to a Merrow guard. "Sound the alarm."

Within moments, the fortress bellowed a whale-like horn.

"You come with us," Captain Jonn said to Yeri. They quickly marched to the back of the hall as mermaids and mermen rushed in a frenzy from the approaching monster. Just on the other side of the congregation was a waterhole encircled by a golden banister.

"Duke Lir wants you close, so I'm afraid you'll be accompanying us to the bridge," Captain Jonn explained, pointing to the waterhole. It looked placid and was difficult to see through. "This is a merway to the bridge. Much like the tubes you see all around here. You first."

Yeri gulped at the merway. "I'm very good with stairs, sir. Is there—"

"It's twelve levels down, and we'll be dead by then," Captain Jonn said. "Afraid this is our only recourse." And with that the Merrow captain stiffened his index finger and forcefully tapped Yeri on the shoulder. He tried to grab for the merman's arm as he fell into the water, but the only thing he caught was the captain's smirk.

Nick's wallfly leapt in after Yeri. Surprisingly, the wallfly could breathe and hear underwater.

The merway's current immediately pulled Yeri into the tube, almost sucking out the precious bit of oxygen trapped in his cheeks. The tube quickly turned right and banged him against the side. He lost his oxygen after all. The translucent tube suddenly went gray, and he could tell they were outside the fortress. With a nice straightaway, the merway increased its speed. His arm, skin, and lips began to drag behind him. He put his hands out to slow down (though he really wanted to be out of this ghoulish merway as soon as possible), but the surface felt like glass and was little help to him.

The merway cut left, and everything went from gray to stone black. Yeri's mouth tried to open for a gulp of oxygen. He forced it closed, but his lungs were starting to ache.

The merway whipped him in an almost complete circle, dropped, whipped a second time, then a third, fourth, fifth. Yeri lost count. Meanwhile, lights from outside the tube flashed on, and there were ghostly figures. They disappeared, came back, and disappeared again. This happened over and over. He must have been moving between levels.

Yeri was turned upside down. He looked to his feet, which were now upward, and saw a small light in the distance. He might actually make it out of the bowels of this nightmare fortress alive.

He gulped for air.

Water blew into his lungs.

He gulped a second time.

Water rushed through his nostrils. He pounded the glass, crying out in his mind. He was going to die upside down in this tube.

Like a geyser, the merway flung Yeri through the opening, feet first. He flipped once, landed on his bum, and then fell over, gagging. A large hand slapped him between the shoulder blades, and he coughed out what seemed to be gallons of water.

"You were a little slow," Captain Jonn said, "but not so bad after all. I half expected to be resuscitating you with an airworm. Now, afraid I've got a bridge to look after." He spun around and bellowed. "Forgo port maneuvers, helmsman. Planesman, withdraw ballasts! Right rudder and all ahead flank!"

From somewhere, Yeri could feel the engines growl as the floating fortress leaned hard away from the cliff face and turned.

"Weapons conn," Captain Jonn said. "Engage hex shields. Flank bell, helmsman. Open that throttle. Give it all she's got. Engineering. Status report..."

As Captain Jonn barked out orders to his mermen, Yeri took a second to choke out the last bits of water.

"The next time Jameson asks me to cover his shift," he said, moving to his hands and knees, "the answer will be undeniably no!"

He slowly climbed to his feet, trying to orient himself, but it proved to be difficult. The only thing separating the ocean from the bridge were sheets of glass divided up by iron beams. Through the glass, he could see a 360° panoramic view of the underwater ocean. Yeri walked slowly toward the view. Powerful fortress lamps cast an indigo light, making the water look smoky and melancholic. If there was some kind of underwater threat out there, he couldn't see it.

"Release the lumens," Captain Jonn said. "Eighty-five percent."

"Releasing the lumens," several voices repeated the order.

Click, click, click came the sound of hatches opening below deck. Thousands of jellyfish, as small as apples and as bright as the noonday sun, shot from the fortress into the dark waters. The ocean bloomed with the lumens, making it look like a sea of stars. They lit the underwater plainly. Yeri could see mountain ridges and their canyons to the east, a forest of kelp running along the cliffs to the west, and a hundred yards away, two waterdragons staring back at them.

Yeri whimpered.

The water dragons were unlike land dragons in that they were wingless and had an eel's body. But they were like land dragons in that they shared the same wicked faces with their sliver black eyes and hyena-shaped head. Also, they breathed fire.

The waterdragons' nostrils looked to be lava pits, and their teeth resembled the gates to the very heart of Mount Kenova. The waterdragon on the left seemed to have blue fire in its craw, while the dragon on the right had yellow fire. Dujinnin were saddled on the back of the beasts. They wore a breathing contraption and held reigns harnessed to black metal helmets with ram-shaped horns. Those horns must have been what had smashed into the fortress earlier.

Yeri turned to Captain Jonn to inquire about a bathroom *immediately*, but the captain could not be found among the chaos. What he did see were several Merrow officers rushing around. One officer stood in the middle of the bridge gripping a wheel. Above him, large pipes dropped from the ceiling to several unmanned stations. At the far end were stacks of barrels lashed down, and an assortment of differently shaped canons and projectiles. Several hatches, merways, and portholes went to nondescript places.

Two cylinders with the word "engines" painted on the front lay parallel to each other. Directly behind the engines and outside of the fortress, two gargantuate-sized propellers churned the water.

Captain Jonn appeared behind Yeri with a short, freckle-faced officer.

"Sir," the officer said to Captain Jonn. "We have the Dujinnin at bay for the moment. Ensign Thrikly cast a repealer. A well executed hex if I do say so myself. Should give us enough time to escape if the furnaces are held to maximum."

"Tell me, Quartermaster Tiggs," Captain Jonn said. "Was Ensign Thrikly on his fourth harjuice of the evening?"

Quartermaster Tiggs slowly opened his mouth and then closed it. He looked like a beached fish.

"Then he was drunk beyond measure and performed a terrible hex. We have minutes before they break through." Captain Jonn said.

"We could try for a phantom hex and be gone before they know it," Quartermaster Tiggs offered.

"Prancing and parlor tricks," Captain Jonn shot back. "We must *kill* the waterdragons."

Quartermaster Tigg's eyes grew. "Very—very well, sir. I know we've got a humling on board, but we cannot—" He glanced quickly to Yeri, then back to the captain. "We cannot do it dry. We're too slow, sir. These contraptions are good for politicians, not battles."

"On that you are correct," Captain Jonn said, looking at their automalegs. "We need to flood the compartment. Very sorry, Yeri."

"Excuse me?" Yeri looked at Quartermaster Tiggs and Captain Jonn.

"We must be able to swim freely to fulfill our duties," Captain Jonn said. "Our automalegs are no good in an underwater battle. We will need to fill the bridge with water."

"But I cannot breathe underwater!" Yeri said.

Captain Jonn looked to a station to his left, "Flood the bridge!"

The officer nodded and spun a wooden wheel several revolutions. Tiny holes from floor to ceiling opened up and showered the compartment. The merways and hatches erupted with water.

"Sir!" Yeri called after Captain Jonn, already walking through a foot of water. "I am without gills!"

Quartermaster Tiggs trudged away and quickly returned with a small chest. It bobbed up and down in the rising water.

"What say you, Captain Jonn," Quartermaster Tiggs nodded to Yeri, trying to yell over the spraying water. "Migarees?"

"I don't think he could stomach the pint of larvae worms," Captain Jonn said.

The water licked at Yeri's calves.

"Jellied troll fat?" Quartermaster Tiggs said, opening the chest and rummaging through it.

"Afraid not, Tiggs. Doesn't have the build for it,"

Captain Jonn said. "His heart would blow up to the size of a pig's bladder."

The water had risen to Yeri's waist.

"Ah. Mulmouse venom for sure," Quartermaster Tiggs said.

"The shakes and the vomiting would take an hour at least. We do not have the time."

"You are right, of course," Quartermaster Tiggs said, "Besides, I believe he is partial to his fingernails. They are well manicured. I don't think he'd like them melting off. Might I suggest obmorcrabs then, sir?"

"How do you feel about obmorcrabs?" Captain Jonn yelled to Yeri.

"Oh quite tasty, sir," Yeri nodded, the water now to his chest. "Especially smothered in laromi sau—"

"Good," Captain Jonn said as he grabbed the back of Yeri's head, reached into the floating chest, and raised up the belly of a living obmorcrab.

Yeri flinched. Its underside had two roaming tendrils, two throbbing suckers, and a mass of smaller tendrils near its belly.

He shoved the crab onto Yeri's face.

He thrashed in the rising water as the obmorcrab wrapped around his head. Two cold tendrils slithered down his eardrums, and the suckers sealed around his eyes, making it impossible to blink. The mass of smaller tendrils ran down his mouth and nose. He choked from the feeling of hundreds of worms filling his chest. He thought swallowing salt water was bad enough, but now his lungs were being filled with crab appendages.

Captain Jonn yanked Yeri underwater and, strangely enough, spoke to him, "Breathe, Yeri. Just breathe."

Yeri tried to rip off the crab, but it squeezed harder. His arms flailed, and he reached for the surface only to find that the bridge was completely flooded. Finally, with no other alternative, he took a breath.

It might as well have been a spring day in Gromwell village. He could breathe deeply and fully. In fact, the bridge looked and sounded even better than before. The only difference was it felt like all gravity had been removed, letting him float around.

"Obmorcrabs were born without the ability to see or breathe underwater," Captain Jonn said, "but their food sources dwell ocean below. They use host bodies such as land mammals and you humlings to travel through the ocean. For the Merrows' sake and yours, they make it much easier for you to breathe underwater and communicate with us, as I am doing now. No worries, Yeri. It is not permanent."

Yeri turned his crab-face to Captain Jonn. "But it is perfectly horrifying, isn't it?"

The captain smiled, unbuckled his automalegs, and swam to the captain's chair. Lir quickly zipped out of a merway and asked the captain for a status report. While they were conferring, a ring of light flashed outside the fortress.

Captain Jonn looked up. "And our only outer defenses just went away. As I said, Officer Thikly's repealer was useless. Helmsman Fraymouth. Mark your head."

"Two, five, three," said an olive-skinned merman.

"Dive sixty feet, mark two, five, six," Captain Jonn said. "Comm. Alert the fortress. We're going full submersion."

The waterdragons tucked back and sped outside the lumens' light.

"Look, Captain," Yeri said with a touch of hope. "The waterdragons flee."

"They do not flee," Captain Jonn said. "They join."

"Joi—?" Yeri started to say when the waterdragons reappeared twisting around each other like two ropes. They were rushing the fortress.

"Brace for impact!" Captain Jonn said.

Horns and snouts slammed the glass. The fortress shuttered, but the glass remained intact. The waterdragons whipped around and disappeared a second time.

"Not enough to break through," Yeri chuckled to himself.

"They were testing our defenses," Lir explained. "Trying to assess our hexes. We have fourteen currently active ones. But they're not done with us. The waterdragons travel with their mates for a reason. The male's fire is blue, the female's yellow. Separately, neither fire can penetrate our hexes, but when they join their fire together, the sun itself would be hewn in two."

Two points of light were spinning around each other in the distant ocean, a blue and a yellow one. The lights increased in size until Yeri could see the flames. The waterdragons were breathing fire as they spun. Blue flames rolled into yellow, and yellow whipped into blue until the flames were a fiery emerald.

"Left full rudder, helmsman," Captain Jonn said.

"Left full rudder," Helmsman Fraymouth repeated. The sound of bending metal came as the fortress leaned heavily to the left.

"Tactical. Speak to me," Captain Jonn said.

"Distance to collision," Officer Thrush called out. "Starboard. Two hundred yards."

The combined dragons' fire cut a swath through the horde of lumens, igniting the jellyfish like firecrackers on Midsummer's Eve.

"Weapons. Ready sirenchaffs," Captain Jonn said.

"Readying sirenchaffs," called a sailor.

"Distance to collision," Officer Thrush said, "one hundred yards."

Yeri could now see a ring of bubbles around the dragon fire; the water boiled frenetically and angrily.

"Chaff ready, sir," called a sailor.

"Distance to collision," Officer Thrush said, "thirty yards."

The glass began to steam with the dragons' heat. The metal braces whined, threatening to unsnap and shatter the glass. Yeri looked to Captain Jonn, whose right hand bobbed in the water as his hair wormed freely. What was he waiting for?

"Distance to collision," Officer Thrush said, "thirteen yards. Ten yards. Eight ya—"

"Launch sirenchaffs," Captain Jonn ordered.

"Launching sirenchaffs," the sailor called back.

Three cigar-shaped iron pods with small propellers ejected from somewhere below and toward the waterdragons. The mechanical decoys emitted a low, melodic sound, almost putting Yeri to sleep instantly. The musical decoys swept just past the head of the waterdragons, who immediately curled around and followed after. The Dujinnin riders tried to steer their beasts back on course, but they wouldn't be altered.

"Sirens are waterdragons' main source of food," Quartermaster Tiggs said. "Their song might as well have been a call to dinner. Our phono-recorded ones make a fine alternative."

The waterdragons continued to spin toward their own tail. So taken were they by their decoy that they forgot to stop breathing their green fire. The flames cut right through their tails and ran up their backs. While they were thrashing wildly, the two Dujinnin riders tried to eject, but weren't quick enough.

Captain Jonn released a long held breath, "I think that will—"

A leviathan appeared.

Yeri's stomach melted as gasps swept around the bridge.

"Dear Möon," Captain Jonn said.

The great sea monster filled the entire view at the rear of the ship. Lumens cast thousands of lights across its face, which was armored in a bony plate. The plate was made up of thousands of incisor teeth. It had a large midsection that edged the ocean's floor and surface. Bolted into its cranium was an enclosed iron carriage. It seemed to be a deck from where the Dujinnin controlled their beast. Yeri could see several men holding reigns that were harnessed to its head, arms and legs.

"Reverse engines!" Captain Jonn yelled. "Full reverse!"

Sailors and officers exploded into action. Mermen swam by and water swirled, as the bridge did everything they could to put some distance between the fortress and the impossibly large monster.

Quartermaster Tiggs swam past Yeri, saying to himself, "Monster will just crush us against the cliffs."

The engines moaned as they were put into full use. The fortress turned sharply, and the leviathan's face angled away as its orbish eyes tracked their movement.

"We must abandon ship, Duke," Captain Jonn said.

"We cannot leave this ship," Lir said. "You saw what the fouls did to my brother-in-law and sister. They will not stop until we've all been infected."

"Then what are your orders?" Captain Jonn said.

Lir paused and then said to himself, "We'll be the decoy. Bearing three, two, nine, helmsman. Dive twenty-three feet, then rudder amidships. A straight line away. Let it chase us."

Helmsman Fraymouth confirmed the order and

sent it down. The fortress was surprisingly nimble for its size. Within moments, they were quickly out of the lumen's light range and in the dark open sea. They could only hope the leviathan was of the slow sort.

"May I, Captain?" Lir said, pointing to the captain's chair.

"The most decorated captain of the nine seas? Of course, Duke," Captain Jonn said. The mermen traded places.

Lir swung his chair and faced the churning propellers. He called out, "Ensign Prymus, bow lights. Let's see if it's chasing us."

Twenty lamps flickered on, and Yeri could see the wicked reflection of the leviathan's eyes between the propellers. The monster was keeping steady... he changed his mind. It wasn't keeping steady, it was gaining on them.

"They've got a quick one," Captain Jonn said.

"Good," Lir said. "Engine room. Prepare for Jasper maneuver."

The sailors stopped their activity for a moment, the tension palpable, but then resumed. This was Duke Lir after all.

The leviathan's snout came into view, the lamplights reflecting its bony shell. The shell's edges were covered in barnacles and mollusks.

"Distance to collision," Officer Thrush said, "fifty yards."

"Engine room," Lir said. "On my mark, invert propellers twenty degrees. We must time this right, mer-men."

"Distance to collision," Officer Thrush said, "twen-ty-three yards... twenty-one yards... eighteen yards... seventeen, sixteen, fifteen, fourte—"

"Invert propellers!" Lir commanded.

A dull noise came from the engines, and the pro-pellers turned toward each other. The whirling bubbles now concealed the bottom part of the leviathan's jaw, but its black eyes still peered over the churning water.

"Nine yards," Officer Thrush called. "Eight. Seven. Six."

Lir pounded his fist. "Eject propellers!"

Two sailors gripped floor levers and pulled with their entire body. Both propellers burst from the rear of the ship and flew out like runaway buzz saws. The leviathan flinched upward to move away from the projectiles, but all it did was expose its neck. Its head shredded away, and the beast spun in a greenish bloom of its own blood.

Sailors jumped up from their posts with cheers and shouts as the monster and its bridge sunk down into the darkness. Yeri thought he saw something shoot out of the sunken bridge, but he was overtaken by a very happy Quartermaster Tiggs.

"Engage auxiliary engines," Captain Jonn ordered, then turned to Lir. "Fine work, sir, fine work indeed."

"I only wish we'd had another option," Lir said. "Without our propellers, we're dead in the water. Only our auxiliary engines to limp along by. And there's still a foul on board.

"Right," Captain Jonn said.

"I saw them," Lir said. "More were on the bridge of the leviathan. So was their leader. We're trapped in our own fortress."

"Right," Captain Jonn said again. "We still have the Steward of Huron."

"And a way to reach him." Lir turned to Yeri. "Our stagecoach driver could get word to him."

"I could what?" Yeri said.

"The fouls cannot smell you, Yer— "

Suddenly, the sound of glass broke, the lights went out, and the cries of joy turned into screams. Near where the propeller had been ejected, Yeri could see a shattered window and the shadow of some hulking monster with thousands of red eyes. It looked like the same shadow that had chased them from Gromwell village.

"We've been breached!" Captain Jonn yelled. "The fouls made their way in after all. Quarantine the bridge. Seal all exits!"

Mermen were screaming and clawing at their skin as the shadow moved toward the front of the bridge.

"Get Yeri out of here before he sees this," Lir said. "He must take the oath first. Take him to the duke's chamber."

Before Yeri could make out the creature, Captain Jonn spun him again and locked eyes. "I don't know if I will ever see you again, stagecoach driver. So I will say this. I can see the goodness in your heart. You must save us, Yeri. You must help us get word to the outside. We need the

Steward of Huron."

Captain Jonn yanked the obmorcrab off Yeri's face and pushed him down a merway for the second time that day.

All along the way he heard the captain's words: *"You must save us, Yeri. You must help us get word to the outside. We need the Steward of Huron.*

Kevin Rayfield McGill

Chapter Ten
Oaths & Agatha

Lyons?" Yeri grumbled to himself as he crawled out of a merway, which led to a bridge and a pool. "What do they mean, I must get word to Nikolas Lyons? A Steward of Huron nonetheless. I'm a driver, not a messenger. How did I get caught up in all this mess? This has gone too far. I must tell them that. I need my horses, and I need to be off. All of Gromwell village will be looking for me by this time."

He smacked his head a couple of times, trying to bang out the water, but it was hopeless. He climbed onto the large white bridge that turned out to be a whale's backbone, which spanned the breadth of the water. Where was he again? Oh, right. The Duke's chambers, though it really wasn't a chamber at all, but a pool, the whalebone bridge being the only dry surface.

Yeri's attention was caught by some kind of movement in the pool. There were strange sea creatures stirring beneath. They were a bit monstrous, a bit mysterious, and altogether fascinating.

A pair of mermaids broke through the water's surface and grabbed two silver cords. Like a harpist's gentle stroke, they pulled the cords down until a platform emerged. On it were two ornate thrones, the occupants being Duke Lir and his wife, Nia.

Yeri was about to say something when he saw Lir's face buried in one hand while gripping Nia's other hand. He could hear the merman's quiet sobs.

"I'm—I'm sorry," was all Yeri could manage.

"Afraid we've lost many lives today," Nia said with a sad expression directed at her husband. "First his brother and then over half the sailors on the bridge."

"Oh dear," Yeri said. "They didn't make it? Captain Jonn?"

"Many perished," Nia said, "but Captain Jonn survived."

A group of black-robed mermaids slowly rose out of the pool. One mermaid began to sing a lonely, quiet note, the beginning of a mournful song. After a few verses, the rest of the singers accompanied her. Their words were in a language Yeri did not recognize; he did recognize the tone, however. The Merrows mourned for their fallen.

After they finished, Lir breathed, regained his composure, and sat up. "Leave us now, Nia. Your mother is right. You're in no condition."

"I cannot leave you at this hour." Nia's hand was interlaced with Lir's. "The headaches will pass."

"Forgive my rudeness," Yeri called out. "What is all this business? I've been in the dark far too long. What are these foul creatures? Who are the Dujinnin? And what happened to your brother? As senior driver of Fungman, Zedock, and Josiah, I demand an explanation this very moment."

"If we were to tell you," Lir said, "you would be put under the strictest of oaths, one that would require your very life."

"My very life?" Yeri's tone quickly shifted from demand to farewell. "I will be on my way, then. Very sad you've run into trouble, but it's got nothing to do with me and my horses. Good day, your Grace and... er, Grace-ess."

Pain, deep and bottomless, filled Nia's eyes. "Please, Yeri Willrow. Do not leave us. You are the Merrows' only call for salvation. Our enemies mean to exploit our weakness and will do so if none will speak for us."

"So... I, well—" Yeri's heart turned doughy. He never could manage himself around a beautiful woman, even the half-aquatic sort. But he couldn't give in now to his weaker emotions. Every minute he stood on this whalebone platform was a minute closer to his doom; he felt it. The stagecoach driver collected the words that would inform Nia he had to leave, no matter what. Nothing could be done. He had to just simply say no.

He opened his mouth... and chickened out, "Well... I... the—the Dujinnin. Are they from Huron?"

"They are a people from the Oruse Isles," Nia removed a pinch of stardust from a satchel and flung it into the air. She whipped her fingers and an image of a light brown-skinned man appeared. He had dreadlocks to his waist, thick facial features, and looked entirely unpleasant.

"I am afraid we are the cause of their hatred for us," Nia continued. "For over one thousand years, we enslaved their entire race. We treated them no better than cattle, worse even. While it has been a long time since they gained their freedom under Huron's instruction, they've never forgiven us. They wish to bring us to our knees."

"Are they after your treasure?" Yeri said. "You have bits of treasure tucked here and there? As the old tavern toads tell it anyway."

"Yes." Nia's hand glided along the silicon armrest. "Very observant, Yeri. It is about the treasure; it's always about the treasure. You are familiar with sulmare? The most precious metal of Earth and Möon? Merrows have been endowed with the gift of sulmare-making."

Nia rubbed her fingers, giving the universal sign for money. Three sulmares sparked into existence and clinked into her open palm. She flung them at Yeri's feet.

"I'll be…" Yeri held up the sulmare, mouth agape. The coins were still hot from Nia's making. They felt rough and smooth, heavy and light, all at the same time. These three pieces would feed him and his mother for a month.

"Because every Merrow is endowed with the power of sulmare-making, we are tasked with its protection and distribution, both here and on Earth. Merrow fortresses patrol all coastlines, protecting the sulmare banks. Lir and I were charged with the Eynclaene offshore accounts."

"They want your abilities of sulmare-making?"

"Not entirely. Our money is secondary. They want revenge. They mean to expose our—" Nia stopped to looked at her husband, then back to Yeri. "Tell me, Yeri. Have you ever visited the fair city of Huron?"

"Of course, ma'am. Who hasn't? We go at least once a year. I've a fine map of it hanging on my bedroom ceiling. Know every borough, alleyway, and byway. My father was born there, you know, Möon rest his soul," Yeri paused. "Anyway. Yes, in short."

"Permit me one more question," Nia said. "Are you a hero, Yeri?"

"A hero, my lady?" Yeri slipped the three sulmares into his knee breeches.

"Yes. Have you ever heroed?"

"Well, uh, er, I mean, Father thought I showed promise, but schooling was a trifle expensive, and there wasn't one to apprentice me. And now—" Yeri rubbed a slightly bulging tummy. "—afraid I'm not quite in the condition for heroism."

"Would you like to be one?"

"Agatha would like it."

"Agatha?"

"Yes," Yeri said, "Agatha is my sweetheart. But she won't marry me on the account of, well, my belly, to be honest. She will marry nothing less than a hero. And Agatha made it quite clear that a hero does not have an "amorphous midsection." Afraid I'm destined to live out my days with Mother."

"I need a hero of high quality to take a message to the Huron City Council," Nia said. "It must be someone who is not Merrow, one whom the fouls cannot smell."

"Oh... well, honestly, ma'am, it being the holidays and all... and, er, my dear mum. I mean, I... forgive me. When you asked for my help, I imagined a ride free of charge or a lent horse. But all this? More than I can handle. Gromwell doesn't see too much in the way of adventure. Once, when I was no bigger than a leviathan's pimple, there was the scourge of the three-headed chicken. It was a bit frightening at first. One head breathed fire; the other two breathed chicken feed and pond water. But it turned out when the first two heads spewed out fiery chicken feed, the last one would put it out. Counterproductive in the end, really."

Nia leaned in. "Agatha, right? Well, Yeri. If you take on this quest, you will trim up that hero's physique within the month."

"Truly?"

"Truly."

Yeri's gaze drifted. He saw Agatha's flirtatious eyes flash across his view and then those soft lips whispering the word "marriage." Yeri clapped his hands. "Always wanted to holiday in Huron, m'lady!"

Nia smiled and reached out to her husband. "Love. The greatest motivation."

Lir squeezed her hand and immediately picked up a squid pen and scroll. "Because our kind guards the treasure of the brother worlds, we carry a special citizenship under the city of Huron, and with it, the protection afforded her citizens. The Merrows are in need of that protection. Within this scroll is a secret to which only Merrows are privy. Our enemies, the Dujinnin, have discovered it and mean to exploit this secret. If we are exposed, it will destroy all Merrow kind. I now entrust this secret to you and to the Steward of Huron, Nikolas Lyons. He sits on the city council under the Roggen Tree. In case the scroll is lost, I'm afraid we must divulge this secret to you, also, so you may pass it onto the steward.

"On that, we must have full assurance you will not betray us, Yeri." Lir removed a large, white pearl from a small satchel and handed it to a guard. The guard's automalegs swiveled around, and he walked up the whalebone bridge and toward Yeri.

Lir's voice dropped. "This is a pearl-of-devotion,

Yeri. It will rest itself in the lining of your stomach. If you betray our secret, this pearl will turn your skin to algae and your insides to seaweed. It will be a long, painful death, to be sure."

The guard came within inches of Yeri's face. He looked down at the iridescent skin of the merman's fingers and the pearl-of-devotion that was to sit in the lining of his stomach. Something like a conscience reminded the stagecoach driver he was about to take *another* oath. Was this really a good idea?

With a sigh, Yeri picked up the pearl. "Big bugger, isn't it? Heh, heh."

"If you are loyal to our kind," Lir said, "then take, Yeri, and swallow."

"A bit of harjuice?" Yeri asked the guard. "Or maybe a swallow of harchoco to wash it down?"

The guard's face remained stolid.

"Right. I see." Yeri nodded. With a sigh, he set the pearl-of-devotion between his molars, hoping it was chewable.

Krrekkkk.

It wasn't chewable.

So, with watery eyes, Yeri swallowed.

"Now," Nia breathed in deeply, "you may read the message."

Yeri bit his bottom lip as he slowly unscrolled the seaweed parchment.

To Your Honor, Steward of the City of Huron and its surrounding provinces, Nikolas Lyons. This document contains the folly of the Merrows.

Yeri began reading out loud, "This secret is the shame of our kind." He choked on the next words. "Here—here is the abominable truth, Steward Nikolas Lyons."

Nick's wallfly swept closer so that it could hear everything. It buzzed past a guard, who flinched. Just as Yeri read the words "we are", the guard smacked the wallfly, and it flew into the Merrows' pool.

Kevin Rayfield McGill

Chapter Eleven
A Question For The Road

Minutes passed while Nick's wallfly thrashed to get out of the water. Finally, it flew out just as he heard Yeri say, "must save the Merrows, or we will surely perish. This terrible secret will be our undoing if left to the Dujinnin." He continued to read Lir's message out loud. "Please Steward, send aid. You are our means of salvation."

Nick couldn't believe it! Even though the wallfly could breathe underwater, he couldn't hear Yeri over its thrashing. He'd missed the Merrows' secret completely.

Yeri looked slowly to Lir and Nia while rolling up

the scroll. "This is a tragedy, my lady. I will secure this... to my very heart."

"No humling or creature has ever known our secret, until now," Nia said. "You understand why the pearl-of-devotion was so necessary."

The guard took the scroll from Yeri and returned it to Lir. Another attendant held out a large fish scale with a puddle of steaming red wax. Lir rolled up the scroll, lifted the scale, and poured the wax over the edges of the paper. He raised a signet ring and with a commanding tone said, "Be ye the hand of the Steward Nikolas Lyons or be ye the hand that turns black and dead." A hundred strands of black swarmed between the signet ring and the scroll. He pushed the ring over the flap. The wax sizzled and transformed into glass, sealing the scroll.

"Remember," Lir said, "only Nikolas Lyons may read this."

"Of course, Duke," Yeri said as he took the scroll from the attendant. The senior stagecoach driver felt a new emotion creep up his spine. He hoped it wasn't courage. Yes, he wanted a hero's physique that might catch the eye of Agatha, but he didn't want to give over to heroism. Mum had always said, "Do not try to be a hero, Yeri. You'll just get someone killed, probably yourself."

"Please, Yeri," Lir said. "Follow the attendant down-stairs."

Nia gently pressed her hand on Lir's arm. "My body

has betrayed my will. I must rest now."

He nodded to an attendant, who quickly brought a velle to the tired duchess.

Yeri could hear the ocean water break between the floating fortress and cliffside. The only thing that kept him from plummeting down to his death was a thin plankway leading to the cliff, on which he currently stood. Yeri took the last step and exhaled. Lir and Captain Jonn followed slowly with the help of their automalegs. Having crossed, all three were now outside of the fortress and walking down crude steps hewn into the cliff. After a few minutes of descent, they entered a cave. The only sign of life was a lamp dangling over the stern of a small boat at the edge of a pool.

"In the boat you will find enough provisions to last you two weeks," Lir said. "This pool leads to a merway, much like the ones you've seen in the fortress, except this particular one is not completely submerged, allowing for humling travel."

Yeri looked again. Sure enough, at the far end of the pool was a watery tunnel.

"The water is enchanted, carrying you inland and along the merway. This merway cuts through the Dorseteen cave system and will take you four hundred miles west to Fendrow county. There you will find a blacksmith by the name of Mullen. She will know you by the signet. Simply say, 'squall,' and Mullen will provide you with a horse and a few week's rations. Do not forget.

Now, once you row down the merway, you will not be able to return. We must undock from this port for our own protection. If you have questions, now is the time to speak."

"It's a bit dark in there, isn't it?" Yeri's voice reverberated down the tunnel. "Those monsters couldn't make their way down there, right?"

Lir clutched Yeri's bony shoulder. "You are our only means of salvation, Yeri Willrow."

Yeri nodded.

"Do you have any other questions?" Lir said.

"None that I can think of, Duke." Yeri shook his head.

Secretly, he wished he had a myriad of questions—anything to stall the inevitable. He sighed, reached out to Captain Jonn's muscular forearm, and awkwardly placed his left foot over the boat. He lifted the oar but didn't drop it into the water.

"I do have a question, Lir, if you'll forgive me," Yeri said. "Anyone might call himself a steward. How can I tell one from another?"

"Every city speaks to her steward."

"Very good." Yeri did not drop the oar. "One more thing. He could simply lie and claim the city speaks to him?"

"That is why the scroll has been enchanted and will recognize the true Steward of Huron from a false one." Lir nodded.

"Right. Very good..." Yeri still did not drop the oar. "One last thing. It seems I've already forgotten his—"

"Lyons. His name is Nikolas Lyons."

"Read my mind, sir. Thank you, sir."

Yeri slowly dropped the oar and pushed away. As the water squeezed into the frothing merway, he began practicing his introductory greeting to the great Steward of Huron:

"Greetings, oh fair Steward Nikolas Lyons.

"*Steward* Nikolas Lyons.

"*Hello,* Nikolas Lyons. The Merrows need you to save them if you please.

"Sir Steward *Nikolas Lyons,* the Mermen are in *grave* peril.

"*Oh,* gracious, excellent, Steward Nikolas Lyons, you must save the Mer—"

At that moment, the wallfly must have been swept underwater because the recording faded away. Nick was now looking inside the memory-in-a-bottle and a miniature version of Yeri going down the tunnel.

He pulled the bottle away. It felt like he'd been in the world of Möon for days. It took a moment to adjust himself, like after waking up from some dream or reading a really good book.

He turned the bottle upside down, and the wallfly tumbled out into his hand. The still figures in the bottle disappeared.

He looked slowly to Grand. There was a crick in his neck from staring in the bottle too long, and his throat was dry. Slowly, he opened his mouth and said through a crackly voice, "The mermaids... Grand. I have to save the mermaids."

Chapter Twelve
Trackers

Mermaids?" Tim shook his head, looking at Nick and then Grand. "What's wrong with you two? There's no such thing as mermaids."

Nick wanted to agree with Tim. Mermaids don't exist. But what had he just seen? The merman and the moon forgotten? All of them walking on automalegs and fighting off strange monsters? That couldn't have just been some advanced virtual reality system, right?

But why should Nick believe Grand? They didn't really even know him. For years their grandfather had been away on special projects. He never told Nick and Tim what he was doing. All he knew was their grandfather had spent most of his time in Machu Picchu. And he definitely never came groundside. He had confided in Nick that a darkness dwelled on the surface. Sometimes he used the word "tracker." Nick just assumed he'd gotten into trouble with the law.

Grand always seemed to get into trouble with someone.

Was he seriously considering what Grand was saying? I mean, he talked to himself a lot, as if he could hear voices in his head. The brothers had just assumed he was losing his mind. Remembering this made Nick a little nervous. Hadn't he just heard a voice in his own head telling him about some evil Rones?

Oh no. Nick thought. *I'm going insane too, just like Grand. Must be genetic.*

"Sorry, Grand, but the joke's over." Tim crossed his arms. "Nice try."

"I explained all of this to you," Grand said to Nick, his voice rising in agitation. "Have you not been getting my messages? That you're THE STEWARD OF HURON? THE MAGICAL CITY BACK ON THE MOON!?"

Nick looked slowly to his left. Several of the patients were beginning to adjust uncomfortably in their seats as the crazy old man declared that his grandson was the destined leader of a magical Moon city. They were probably wondering how long he'd been off his medication.

"Um, Grand," Nick lowered his voice, hoping his

grandfather would take the cue. "The memory-in-a-bottle was a cool bit of tech, but come on. Mermaids on the Moon?"

Grand sighed. "I see there's a good deal more that I need to explain." He had his hands up. "But now is not the time. Where are your parents... and why are we in this hospital?" He said, realizing where they were.

"One moment they were talking, and the next Dad couldn't breathe and turned all purple death. Mom and Dad are in there." Nick pointed to the disease and poison ward.

"They were poisoned?" Grand's eyes grew.

"Yeah," Nick said. "Something about their diet sodas."

"Did they find us?" Grand said, looking to the door with a sign clearly marked: *Disease and Poison Ward: No admittance beyond this point without clearance.*

"The trackers are here in Colorado City!" Grand declared. "We must get all of you out of here, now!"

He tried to pry the doors open. They beeped a warning but wouldn't budge. Then something very strange happened. Their grandfather's eyes lost their hue and turned blue while waves of blue poured from his fingertips.

"Grand?" Nick took a step back. "Um, why are you all blue and misty?"

"It's my jynn'us."

Their grandfather's fingers formed a hollow circle, and he plunged them into the crack of the door. It rolled apart like paper.

He gasped, "The trackers!"

There was a distinct growl from the other end of the door. Nick peered under Grand's arm, expecting to see a couple of mangy dogs.

His stomach flipped.

At the end of the hallway were three monsters. They looked like exiles from the land of where nightmares went to die. All three seemed to have the body of a raptor crossbred with an anorexic hyena, and a face that could've taken the crown for Miss U.S. of Ugly Pageant.

"They found us!" Grand let the doors slam into place. "This was all a trap, Huron!" He looked down to Nick and grabbed his right shoulder. "The trackers don't want you to return home. They are bent on stopping us, on stopping you, Nikolas.

Now, it is time we were leaving, boys. Let's go!" Iron-like hands seized their shoulders and shifted them away. He mumbled something about "my scent" as they passed through the waiting room doors. Just as the doors slid closed, Nick heard a crash from the waiting room followed by screams.

"Run!" Grand ordered.

They sprinted out of the hospital and toward the truck. Shouts of terror came from the hospital. Doctors, nurses, and even older patients were piling out of doors and windows.

"In the truck!" Their grandfather commanded.

"Don't dawdle."

The hovertruck's nose was buried in a mulberry bush, clearly ignoring the parking pads. Both boys tumbled into the cab and were met with the smell of pipe smoke and sweat. Before they could manage their harnesses, the hovertruck rocketed upward and in complete defiance of all commercial airway regulations. They sped past a pair of holosigns that read: *Beauty and the Botox: When nature has been beastly to you* and *Mind Transplants: Don't die, download!* Nick glanced quickly at St. Mary's. The monsters were sprinting across the lawn.

"What's going on?" Tim said just as they broke through the clouds.

"It's the trackers," Grand said.

"Trackers?" Nick said.

"I told you about them," Grand said. "You really didn't get any of my messages, did you? We still have much to talk about."

Nick couldn't agree more. The memory-in-a-bottle didn't really answer his questions. Truly, it only produced a hundred more. He still didn't know where he was from, or why they were being chased by three monster-dogs. As if Grand had read his mind, he said, "I'll explain everything to you shortly, boys. I must, Huron. Now is the time!" He pounded his fist on the steering wheel.

They both looked sideways at their grandfather. His crinkled brow spoke worry, even fear. He began bobbing his head. "I'm coming, my love. I'm coming."

Uh oh, Nick thought. *Here he goes again with that mumble-talk.*

"I'm coming. It'll just be a little longer. A few setbacks. Gotta break the trackers scent, but I'm coming, I'm coming, Huron. We must not allow the Merrows to perish. We will save them. I will bring your steward home. We must save them."

"Alright," Grand announced, waking them from their sleep. "This is a good spot."

Nick kicked awake. He didn't know what time it was, but it felt like midnight. He sat up, trying to get his bearings. They were definitely not in Colorado.

"Where are we?" Nick said.

Tim slowly stirred from his sleep. "Is this—?"

"Death Valley," Grand finished his sentence. "We're in California. I need to keep us moving, but I feel like I owe you some kind of explanation about the trackers. I've kept you in the dark for too long."

They jumped out of the hovertruck. Nick stumbled for a moment, the sand shifting under his tennis shoes. He put his hand out and grabbed a bit of the dune to keep himself upright. A gust of wind kicked up, forcing him to cross his arms. He didn't realize deserts could be so cold.

"Now." Grand prodded the inner lining of his coat. "A world of explanations and no time to give them. The trackers are mighty slow by land but know how to get arou—Ah, thought I had a bit of stardust left." He pulled out a purple satchel and tore it open. Iridescent dust flew everywhere. He stuck his hand into the dust and performed several complicated gestures.

"These be the wretched scuccas."

Three monstrous images appeared. The combination of dust and headlights produced a ghostly replica of the trackers. This version moved with their necks to the ground and let out an occasional cry.

The same dread that washed over Nick in the hospital came over him again.

Grand said, "Due to these nefarious beasts, our family has been on the run for fourteen years."

Their grandfather's expression shifted. The fatigue of running for years appeared around his cheeks and brow. With a sigh, he stepped toward the stardust. "They drove us from my fair city, Huron. I forsook my stewardship over her to bring us here, thousands of years in the future." Grand wrung his hands. "Nevertheless, they followed me. It seems that even time and space cannot bind such darkness.

"They are an unnatural kind, filled with dead magic and all its trappings. Scuccas cannot die until they've tracked down and brought their prey to their master. Like a dog or wolf, they can pick up one's scent, but what they do with it is quite wicked. A dog can only smell the trail one leaves behind, but a scucca can smell you, your habits, your passions, your very decisions, present and future. And they will use it against you. That is why they were waiting for me at the hospital.

"You see. It's why I kept to the hovertruck all these years, never coming groundside. Made it difficult for them to pick up a fresh scent. Staying away protected you and your parents from them until... until I got sloppy. For the first time in fourteen years, I let my passions take hold when my archaeological team discovered Ludwig's message. Foolishly, I came groundside, touched Ludwig's chronomessage, and then left it there with the Peruvian. They must have found the artifact and smelled my intentions. Learned of you and your parents. And so the scuccas poisoned them, drawing me to the surface, knowing I would be forced groundside again to fetch your parents."

"Are they the same monsters that were chasing the Merrows?" Nick said.

"No," Grand said. "If you recall, those monsters had thousands of red eyes, and they did something to the Merrows, corrupting them. A scucca cannot do that. Its power is to track. They are two different agents of evil, two different missions, I'm afraid."

"Yeah, OK," Nick said. "Why are they chasing our family?"

"Someone wanted to remove me from power over Huron, to take away my stewardship. I believe the attack on the Merrows is not coincidental. Once they chased our family away, then the city of Huron and her citizens, which include the Merrows, would be left vulnerable."

"How did your leaving make Huron vulnerable?"

"The voice!" Grand shouted. "The city. She speaks to the steward. Many scheme to destroy Huron, so they may rob her of her powerful magic. But she knows, Nikolas. She knows when someone intends evil against her gates. She speaks to the steward, warning him of the coming peril. She will guide you, revealing her enemy's foul schemes. This is why the trackers ran us out of Huron, to leave her vulnerable. Her enemies were tired of being thwarted by the voice at every turn.

The steward must return, so she can tell us how to save the Merrows and defeat the Dujinnin. You, Nikolas, are that steward. *You* must return. If you don't, the Merfolk and your fair city will be destroyed."

"I'm sorry," Tim said. "Did I miss an invitation to the crazy convention? Is this, like, some elaborate joke you two are playing on me?"

"This is no joke, Tim," Grand said. "This is real."

"Real?!" Tim said. "Here are the words that have come out of your and Nick's mouth for the last two hours: 'Mermaids,' 'Moon,' 'magic,' 'agents of evil,' 'time-travel!' Seriously, time travel!? I'm waiting for the part where you actually talk about something REAL!

"Now, I don't know what animals were in that hospital, but shouldn't we call the police or something instead of acting out your crazy role-playing game in the middle of the desert?"

"They weren't animals, they were scuccas, as I just explained to you," Grand said. "And no. We cannot go back right now. We must wait." He sighed slowly. "This isn't fair to you, Tim. It's all too quick. Your parents are gravely ill, you just experienced something very traumatic, and you're in a strange place. I need to give you a little more time to digest all of this."

"Yes," Tim said. "Please allow a few more days, so I, too, can lose my marbles."

Nick didn't say anything, but he wanted to tell Grand to ignore Tim. He had a ga-billion questions to ask him. Like, why was there a voice in his head telling him the Rones were evil, and why did he have a vision of some old-timey city? He really didn't want to wait around for Tim to clue in to what was going on, which, knowing Tim, would be *never*. But Grand was already marching to the hovertruck.

Chapter Thirteen
Going to a Better Place

He'll save the Merrows, Huron. I know he will."

Nick heard the modulator switches kick in as Grand activated the landing gear. The hovertruck began its descent toward a floating electrostation in South Wales. It had been three days since they'd fled the hospital.

"Merrows," Grand mumbled to himself as they pulled into the parking space. "Must save the Merrows. Have to break the tracker's scent first, Huron. You know this. I have to."

The hovertruck landed next to a Pakistani family's van with a trailer hitched to the back. Nick and Tim jumped out and bee-lined it to the convenience store.

"Nikolas," Grand called from the hovertruck. "Be sure to grab three beef jerkies while you're in there."

"What if they have bacon jerky?" Nick said.

"Even better!" Grand said.

Nick nodded and kept walking.

For the past three days, Grand had nearly circum-navigated the Earth. He'd only left the cloud line to eat and use the bathroom.

The flights were long and boring. Most of the con-versations consisted of Tim saying, "We need to go back" or "Mom and Dad might be dead." But Grand remained tight-lipped about their parents. In fact, he'd said very little to the brothers. What was said consisted of: "What will you be eating for breakfast?" "Time for bed now" and "Think we'll see the Himalayans in the morning."

As always, it wasn't what Grand said to *them* that mattered, it was what Grand said to himself. "Have to save the Merrows. Mustn't let the trackers know what I'm thinking, Huron. Keep 'em confused. Break the scent."

Huron? Nick thought to himself as he walked inside the food mart to buy a candy bar. *Grand hears the same voice?*

"Psst," Tim called Nick over, having just grabbed a bag of Sour Powers.

"Yeah," Nick said.

"What's wrong with Grand? Is he getting, you know,

Alzheimer's?" Tim said.

"No." Nick shook his head. "Grand is incapable of illness."

Tim gave a withered look. "Dude. I know you think he's the patron saint of awesomeness or something, but Grand's mind's all screwy. He keeps talking to himself."

"We can drop you off at the nearest daycare if it makes you feel better."

"Just saying that I'm having major doubts about Grand's psychological stability." Tim snatched a bag of jelly beans. "Don't have to be a jerk about it."

"He told us to wait; we wait."

"Since when did you heed the opinion of an authority figure?"

Nick shrugged.

It was true. He didn't care about the opinion of authority figures, except Grand's. He was the only adult Nick had ever respected, which makes sense, since Grand was also the only adult who had ever scared him. It was like someone had taken Aragorn, William Wallace, Beowulf, and mashed them into their grandfather. What do you say to a person like that?

Truly, they'd never had the average grandfather-grandson relationship. Grand never celebrated national holidays with them or Christmas for that matter. He never sent them e-cards with e-money. Grand would send real, physical letters. They were twenty pages long, recording his whereabouts and archaeological activities across the globe, giving full details of the local aviary with samples included. Bat wings. Parrot beaks. Eye and talon of a Sulawesi serpent eagle. It took Nick hours to read the letters because he spent most of the time cross-referencing between Grand's words and the e-dictionary.

Also, Grand never came groundside, so he never had seen where his grandsons lived or went to school. He had always insisted they meet at a Cappumulus, a franchise of coffee shops with locations stationed two miles in the air. More times than not, Grand would carry an oversized axe into the coffee shop, plop it on the counter, and order a large triple espresso, no syrup, no sugar, and no whip. Then he'd fire up his pipe and set off the very sensitive smoke alarms. Most of their coffee sessions entailed Grand grilling Nick and Tim, asking if they had enrolled in any sword dueling classes or at least metallurgy. How many stanzas of poetry had they memorized in the last week, or had they learned to fell a wild animal with their bare hands yet? Tim explained that there were no wild animals within twenty miles of the city limits. Nick reminded himself to download all the books he could find on W. B. Yeats and sword fighting.

Yes. Grand's eccentricities were unnerving, but it was the very reason Nick trusted him. He was as real as they came.

Grand wasn't a drone.

Finally, after another two days of hopping between

electrostations and elevated restaurants, Grand nodded to the ground and said, "That's about long enough."

He punched in a new location: *Grace Church of Colorado City.*

"Church?" Nick said.

"You typed it wrong, Grand. We want to go to St. Mary's," Tim said.

"It's our last chance before they cremate the bodies."

Tim sat up. "Cremate? Mom and Dad are dead?"

Before the truck came to a complete stop, Grand jumped out, reached behind the seats of the cab, and pulled out two antique blowers—the kind their mom and dad kept by the fireside next to the poker and ash scooper. Of course, they never used them since the fire was only a holograph.

Grand took several long strides to the top of the stairs and pulled open the doors. The cobalt blue foyer smelled like a hundred years of perfume, dutifully marching in and out every Sunday.

"They really are dead," Tim whispered, choking back tears.

Grand reached for the sanctuary door.

"Wait," Tim protested. "You can't just march into a funeral service. We're not even dressed for it."

"Erik and Sonya are in there. I am responsible for them."

"Responsible for them?"

Grand opened the door a crack. An air-conditioned

breeze and speaker's eulogy slipped through.

"—will be missed. Sonya was also a good person, a beautiful person. She was a woman in the prime of her days with so much left to give to society. She liked shopping, the reality show, *Laguna Beach Girls,* and—"

Grand flung the sanctuary doors open.

"Grand..." Tim covered his face.

The speaker, a thin man whose scalp majored more on skin than hair, tracked the great old man marching down the aisle.

"Testimonies will be after the rap duet, Mister... ?" The speaker waited for a response he would never get. Grand walked straight to the closed caskets and flipped the lids back like playing cards.

The audience inhaled.

"He's insane!" Nick laughed.

Grand grabbed their mom by the collar and slung her over his left shoulder. He turned a full revolution, her blond hair sweeping around.

Adult voices shouted. "Sonya! Oh no, he's grabbing for Erik, too!"

Teenage voices joined the commentators. "Awesome! No way! That old dude ripped the lid right off!"

Grand heaved their dad onto his other shoulder. He turned to the audience, paused for a moment to steady himself, and then offered his own parting words, "Carry on."

The bodies swayed in beat with Grand's march up the aisle.

"Linus! Say something," a woman hissed from the front row.

Linus' expression could be described as cadaverous.

"Linus!"

"Um—I'm, well, er. Yes, yes. Er—Erik and Sonya have gone to a better place—"

"Linus!" she hissed.

"Well—well, what I mean to say is..."

Grand rolled the bodies to the ground, and Tim closed the sanctuary doors.

"What's going on?" Nick said.

"They're dead!" Tim pulled the locks of his hair. "You just hauled our dead Mom and Dad out of a funeral service—in front of everyone!"

"First, they're not your parents. Second, they're not dead." Grand turned their dad onto his stomach, his nose crunching into the blue carpet.

"Not dead?" Nick looked to Tim.

"They should be, grant you that. Trackers put enough poison in their diet sodas to kill a herd of gwinters. But these are mimes." Grand looked at two very confused boys. "Duplicates, copies. They do appear dead to any modern physician. Nearly on the brink of it, I would imagine. But these particular ones happen to be very difficult to kill. I should know. I bred them that way."

"Bred?" Tim mouthed.

Nick could only stare at what Grand claimed were copies of his parents. Sure, there were moments he had prayed they were not his parents. Especially one after-noon when he invited a bunch of friends to play some *Maverick Seven* on his holobox, and there was his mom doing her Kenpo routine to Baby Gangsta's platinum soundtrack, *A Tale of Two Cribs*. Still, wishing and hav-ing your wish fulfilled are two different things.

"Daniel?" Tim stood up. "Daniel Kobayashi?"

There stood the boy genius leaning on his cane. His hairless, questioning brow said what his mouth could not, *"What the heck is going on?"*

"What're you doing here?" Nick said.

"It's your parent's funeral," Daniel said, in his stacca-to, intelligent tone. "Should we not be in attendance?"

"But they're not your parents," Nick said.

"Are we not friends, Nick?" Daniel said.

"Sure..."

Daniel cleared his throat. "Anyway, Caroline insist-ed we attend. Said you two needed the support of true family during such a loss."

"Oh. My. Gawsh!" Brandy stood in the doorway wearing a black dress, thin black veil, seven-inch black heels, and a matching black purse.

Haley pushed herself around Brandy while Xanthus flanked the left. All were dressed uniformly in black, and all were completely dumbstruck by Grand's body snatching.

"Tim, Nick." Caroline cut through the growing crowd. She flung herself at Tim and then wrapped her other arm around Nick. Her hands were rough and smelled of cherry pie.

"I was so worried." Caroline stepped back. "Are you guys all right?"

"Yeah," Nick said.

"Close the doors," Grand growled.

"That dude just yanked your dead parents from a funeral," Xanthus said, wide-eyed, as he watched Grand push their mom's nostrils up, pull her lips open, and smell a handful of hair.

"What?" Haley said. "Hospital short on cadavers?"

Grand twisted to Haley, then Nick.

"They're my friends." Nick put his hands up. "From the refugee camp."

"Where've you two been?" Haley sidled around Grand.

"Everywhere," Tim said.

"Police couldn't find you," Haley said. "Doing the vanishing act after your parents were poisoned wasn't a great idea. They interrogated all of us, even Rocky the She-Bully. You know she didn't have nice things to say about you, Nick. Told them you were a violent psychopath who burned down forests and punched pretty girls in the mouth."

"We didn't kill them," Nick said. "Besides, they're not dead. Wait. What did you tell them?"

"Nothing." Haley rolled her eyes to Grand, who had his ear to their dad's palm. "Should we have?"

"Seriously," said Xanthus. "What's with William Wallace?"

"That's Grand. He's my grandfather. I told you all ab—"

"Nick, Tim." Grand waved them over. "We need to store them away. Cannot be lugging them all the way to Huron. Bring me the pressers." Grand pointed to the two antique blowers.

Screams peeled from the sanctuary.

Xanthus, nearest to the sanctuary, turned and peaked between the foyer doors.

"Merciful Minerva!" Xanthus turned to Grand. "Bunch of animals chased the pastor off stage."

"Like a bear?" Brandy said.

"No, it's, um..." Xanthus fumbled through his trench coat, mumbling to himself. "Sci... sco... sce..." He pulled out a book titled, *Perlock's Mythological Bestiary: 30th edition.* It looked abused beyond use. He quickly undid the rubber band and started flipping.

"Long neck... wings behind ears... I believe it's a... yeah. Scucca!" Xanthus held the book up to Grand.

"Grand!" Nick said. "He's talking about the trackers."

"Trackers?" Grand shoved the kids aside and placed bluish hands against the foyer doors. "Not again. They thwart us at every turn!"

"Article needs to be seriously updated, though." Xanthus held the book to his nose. "Scales are more heather blue. My bestiary is pretty dated. I prefer the books over the ebooks. Just found them more honest to the source material."

Sounds of a wooden object skidding across a stone floor came from the sanctuary. The screams doubled.

"Dude," Brandy said. "What's with your grandpa's eyes?"

With palms leveraged against the doors, Grand's eyes once again turned blue, and a blue smoke crept from his hands.

"It's his jynn'us," Nick said.

Glass shattered.

Grand turned his glowing eyes on them. "To the truck, all of you. And take the bodies with you, Nikolas!"

Nick couldn't move.

"Now, Nikolas!"

Boom. The sanctuary doors were pushed open, and Grand rocked back. He doubled his effort to keep it closed. The sounds of a clogged vacuum hose came from the other side.

Reeiihh!! A creature sounded the call of recognition and rammed the doors again. Then it began pushing through, sliding Grand backwards. He gritted his teeth, and veins ribboned his neck as he tried to keep back whatever was pushing the doors apart.

"Grab his feet, Nick," Haley ordered.

But Nick couldn't look away from the doors. Something like the belly of a boa constrictor with two slits edged its way in between them. The slits pulsed *grung, grung, grung, grung, grung, grung.*

Grand stood full length. "Gahh!" His fist hammered

the slits. It screamed.

Everyone stopped.

They'd never heard an animal scream like that before. Not the holovids, not the VR zoos, not even the history records. It sounded... other-worldly.

"What was that?" Daniel's eyes grew.

"I told you. A scucca," Xanthus whispered while slowly tucking his bestiary away. "The forces of darkness have descended upon us all. Are we ready?"

Reihhhhh!

"To the truck, already!" Grand reached for the bodies and flung them over his shoulders.

Nick and company exploded through the doors. Daniel leaned on Xanthus while Brandy kicked her platforms down the steps, choosing survival over Louboutins.

Reihhhhh!

Men and women poured out of windows, doors, and any other escape route. The boys scrambled onto the truck bed, and the girls squeezed inside the cabin.

"Here!" Grand rolled the mimes over the lip of the truck bed.

The Erik-mime landed on Xanthus.

"There'sadeadbodyheadonmylap!There'sadeadbodyheadonmylap!There'sadeadbodyheadonmylap!" He tried to squirm away, but the bed gave no place for retreat.

"Where's Brandy?" Haley jumped out of the cab.

"Aiih!" Brandy was sprinting across the lawn, clutching her shoes. She had changed her mind. Louboutins *were* more important than life itself.

"Brandy! Are you crazy!" Haley yelled. "Forget the shoes!"

Glass showered over the lawn, and a blur of lizard skin rolled over. Three monstrous animals found their legs and righted themselves.

"What the –" Haley said.

"What are those things?" Nick stood up on the truck bed.

"I told you, man," Xanthus's voice quivered. "Scuccas. Trackers unto death, our death."

It is a strange feeling to look upon a predator. Your blood doesn't know whether to boil or freeze. Without turning your gaze, you ask yourself, "Should I move? Can it see me?" Inevitably, the predator answers, "Yes." And it always answers the same way: the eyes.

The scucca locked eyes with Nick and screamed. *Reeiihh!!*

Brandy scrambled into the cabin. Grand hit the close and lock button. The hovertruck's thrusters kicked from the ground, whining upward and above the tree line. The tracker covered in chains turned to a red sports car and chomped down onto the wheel. Nick looked back to Daniel, whose fingers were curled over anything that would keep him from tumbling out.

Nick laughed, "Crazy, isn't—"A red car flew inches past his face.

"Woah! Woah!" Nick covered his head.

Metal crashed a beat later. Nick looked down at the scucca, who had locked its teeth onto the wheel of another car.

He pounded on the glass. "They're throwing cars at us, Grand!"

Grand glanced back. "Get your heads down, now!"

The boys wiggled into any position that would keep them below the wall of the truck bed. They pitched right and then left. Black and green flashed over. Nick shoved his fingers into the small lip of the truck bed. All he could do was stare up at the wind whipping around the bed, and wonder what—

A police's hovercycle rolled over. The truck spun. Everyone screamed.

Nick pushed himself up. White smoke fanned over the grill. Grand's forearms crowbarred against the steering wheel, but he couldn't keep the hovertruck from losing altitude.

The truck slammed. Pavement shot it back into the air. Bodies lifted from the bed. It slammed again. Nine hundred pounds of fiberglass and metal skipped across Parsons Avenue and 1125 Farmers Market. Once the hovertruck found road, ground wheels took over.

Grand didn't even consider brakes.

Everyone sat up this time. Nick saw the chained tracker standing in the distance. It lifted onto its hind legs, waiting....

Crack!

The truck spun. Nick's head smacked against the

tailgate. Barely coherent, he looked around with foggy vision. Having just rammed the passenger side door, two trackers rolled over a street meter. They found their legs and sprung to their feet but didn't pursue.

Still, Grand found little use for brakes.

Kevin Rayfield McGill

Chapter Fourteen
The Truth

Having just been downgraded from hover, the truck tore through the first floor of a newly constructed high-rise, two gated communities, and the Colorado City summer parade. The drum major grabbed her skittling baton and yelled after them, "Antique cars will just get someone killed!"

Nick didn't care. He was just happy to put some distance between them and what Grand called trackers.

Eventually, they took the I-45 highway. Since the transportation industry could not afford hover technology, the old highway had been reserved for transport vehicles. Grand was able to zip quickly past the compact trains and eighteen-wheelers.

Once they passed Dickinson Bridge, everyone's leashes began to spark. They shook their wrists, trying to stop the electrical jolts, but it didn't seem to help. BioFarms's properties were moving outside of the assigned fifteen-mile perimeter.

Grand followed the signs to Sion Park. Once there he smashed through the ticket booth's arm guard, ignoring the attendrone's request for payment. With little visibility and a waning Moon that glowed through the Earth's great cloud, they crept along an old service road for another hour. Finally, the truck drove into a forest clearing.

Grand launched from the cab, leaving on the remaining headlight. "This should do for now, Huron. Tried to be as unpredictable as I could. Be patient with me, please, Huron. I'll save the Merfolk, I promise," he mumbled to no one in particular. Grabbing the Erik and Sonya-mimes out of the truck bed, he let them fall like sacks of beef. "Everyone, out."

Haley rushed over to Nick and grabbed him by the arm, "Your grandpa was freaking us out in there," she said. "Kept blabbing on about protecting the mermaids and trackers picking up our scent. Said he'd kill them with his bare hands if he had to. What is going on, Nick? Is your Grand an international criminal or just bonkers?"

"I don't know what's happening." Nick raised his hands.

"My sisters and I can't hang out with a mentally unstable person, OK?"

"OK," Nick said.

Sczaak!! A blue arc leapt around Brandy's leash-band and she whipped her wrist. "Ow! That one really hurt!"

"We've moved out of the refugee camp's range for the leashes," Daniel said.

"Have to figure out how to turn those off," Nick said.

"Don't worry about that. I have a halter." Daniel held a flat object the shape of a dime. "Saved it for such a time. Brandy, your wrist please."

"That's high security stuff?" Nick said.

"Yes. I know," Daniel said. "Brandy. Your wrist, please."

"But the cops don't even have those. Where did you get it?"

Daniel didn't respond. Instead, he held the halter until Brandy's leash clicked and slid to the ground. "Who's next?" Several more wrists raised to Daniel.

"Where did you *get* it, Daniel?" Nick repeated.

"I have my sources," Daniel said.

Nick watched the leashes fall to the ground one by one, their read outs still projecting the refugees' bio-rhythms and life expectancy. Everyone rubbed their wrists while exchanging looks of elation, concern, even wonder. Nick considered the leashes on the ground blinking "Inventory Error." He really didn't understand what it meant to be the property of someone else.

"You and you." Grand pointed to Tim and Xanthus.

"You'll be storing the bodies into the pressers. This is how it's done." He grabbed the pinky of the comatose Sonya-mime and shoved it into the presser's tip. He stepped on the presser and bounced his leg up and down like a one-footed jig. Xanthus's mouth fell open as the Sonya-mime began to shrivel and get sucked into the presser. It was like watching fruit dry. "This presser will keep them for forty-eight hours. After that, they begin to wrinkle. It's a beast getting the wrinkles out."

Tim slowly put one shoe onto the presser. The Sonya-mime's finger slipped out.

"Just shove it back in, Tim," Grand said. "Try the tongue if the finger gives you trouble."

Tim looked at his grandfather like he was seven kinds of insane. He went to his knees, grabbed the red fingernail of the Sonya-mime, and slipped it into the presser. The knuckle crack-popped and slipped out again. Even in the Moonlight, one could see Tim turn pale. After a few more attempts, the finger sealed into place. Tim stood to his feet and began slowly pumping the presser with his foot.

Phfit. Phfut. Phfit. Phfut. The presser blew and sucked.

Grinning at the Erik-mime, Xanthus raised his massive leg and slammed it down.

PHFIT! The Erik-mime jumped a foot.

"Not too hard, now, boy!" Grand yelled. "It'll just make a mess if ya go and pop 'em. Very good, that's more like it. Should keep 'em for the time being,"

Grand sighed. "Have to see about an antidote Möon-side. Now, I'm afraid your friends are about to get a mouthful, Nick. These are the monsters that have been chasing us."

Grand flung a handful of stardust into the air. With a few swirls of his index finger, the scuccas reappeared. Brandy gasped.

Phfuuuuuut. Both pressers stopped sucking.

"Keep pressing, boys," Grand ordered. "We've very little time before the real scuccas are upon us. Now, to catch all of you up."

The pressers beat slowly for the next twenty minutes. *Phfit. Phfut. Phfit. Phfut.* Nick watched Grand re-explain to his friends how the monsters had chased their family away from their home, Möon, and how Nick had to return home to save the Merfolk.

As Grand made large gestures with his massive hands, Nick scanned the faces of all his friends. Daniel tilted over his cane. Haley kept her arms crossed.

Did they believe Grand? Nick thought. *Do I?*

Finally, Grand took a breath and said, "That's about all I told Nick and Tim."

His friends stared back at the wild-eyed man.

Phfit. Phfut. Phfit. Phfut.

Nick hoped they wouldn't laugh out loud at their kooky grandfather.

Phfit. Phfut. Phfit. Phfut.

"I told you it was real!" Xanthus performed a frighteningly good drop-kick. "I told you, I told you. I told you, I told you. No one believed me. No one. Redemption!"

Haley rolled her eyes. "What do they want with you?"

"Bet he's torn between love for his family and duty to his country," Caroline offered.

"Dude. It's gotta be the Lord of Fire and Ice," Xanthus said. "He wants to conscript Grand into his elite warrior guard, but Grand works for *no* one."

"What do they want with you?" Nick repeated Haley's question.

"It's not what they want with me," Grand said, "but what they're trying to keep me from. Chasing me away from Huron has left her and her citizens vulnerable. I believe they were sent by the Dujinnin. The same people who attacked the Merrows. The scuccas kept me on the run these fourteen years, so they could execute their devilish schemes. The Dujinnin have now openly attacked the Merrows. While Merrows—"

"Mermaids?" Xanthus called out.

"Well," Grand said, "that is what we call female Merrows."

"Whatever," Xanthus said. "Mermaids are hot!"

"Anyway," Grand said. "The Merrows do not live within the city walls, but off the coast of Eynclaene in great sea fortresses. Still, they are given Huronite citizenship because they manage and guard all of Huron's wealth in offshore accounts. I would suppose the Dujinnin mean to plunder those treasures. I must return to her and so must you, Nikolas. It is you Huron needs now. I would've never risked coming to the ground and out into the open like this if it wasn't for our dear city. The Merrows are in grave danger and with them, Huron herself. I must bring you home."

"Home?"

"Aye."

Nick couldn't manage a response. All he could do was listen to the pressers. The mimes had withered to half their size.

Grand squared to Nick. "Above all else, what do you desire from this life?"

"To get off this planet," Nick said immediately. He looked at Moon. Without moving his gaze, he continued, "Go home. Moon. But—but I didn't think home was some fantastic moonland."

Nick combed his fingers through his hair. "That's another thing, I don't get any of this. Where's this city you keep talking about? Is there an unheard of civilization on Moon? Underground? Why do you keep talking about the past like you're a time-traveler or something?"

"Because I am," Grand said. "And so are you." He stepped into the middle of the stardust scucca and spun his finger like a lasso, each revolution smaller than the next. Dust began to clot into spheres.

"Saturn... Jupiter... Mars," said Daniel as planets took shape.

"What's that stuff you're using again?" Xanthus said.

"Stardust," Grand said. "This was Earth myriads of years ago, before men kept record of the heavens. If they had, they would have known that our solar system bore not eight, but nine planets." He stepped to Earth and flicked a finger around it. "Earth had a twin."

"Uhhh," the kids breathed in.

A second planet crested over Earth like a blue-white sunrise. But it wasn't its mirror copy, they were fraternals. Slightly larger, its oceans were a deeper hue, its continents more severe and pronounced. And it sparkled, like someone had glazed it over with flecks of glass.

Phfiiiiiiit... The pressers wheezed to a stop again.

"I told you to keep them going, boys," Grand warned Tim and Xanthus. They resumed their pressing.

"Möon was its name," Grand said, "and the brother planets were bound literally one to another."

Nick stepped around Grand for a better look. The planetary bodies were so close that the atmospheres were fused together like Siamese twins. A massive rope crossed the atmospheres, tethering the two planets together.

"The tidal waves?" Daniel shook his head. "The gravitational force between the two would be enough to rip the surfaces apart."

"And so it did, until the tether was constructed by Roch-umbria. It cast a spell over the planets, keeping peace among skies and tides."

"Where's Moon?" Haley unfolded her hands.

"Möon," Nick said, knowing the answer before Haley had asked the question. "Möon *is* the Moon."

"Yes, Nikolas. Well done. Earth, in my time, is nearly inhabitable. Except for the tethered realms, it is ice or wilderness. As fate would have it, Möon, your Moon, is the rich, powerful planet of the brother worlds. Steeped in wonder and mystery, it is the cradle of all magical civilization."

"Dude," said Xanthus, lifting up his bestiary. "Totally makes sense! We have always looked to Moon as our source of magic. Werewolves changed by it, farmers planted their seeds by it, mothers prayed they would give birth by it. Oh, and let us not forget the Greek goddess, Daphne—"

"Hey!" Haley said. "Wanna be sedated? 'Cause I will happily do it."

"It's my job to keep people informed."

"And here—" Grand pointed to the middle of the largest land mass. "—is Huron, home. Your home, Nikolas and Tim."

Tim gave Nick an expression. *Seriously. Is anyone buying this?*

Nick looked at Xanthus, who was furiously taking notes in his bestiary while pumping the presser.

"In my time, the city of Huron is the seat of power on Möon. Huron's magic makes her both the jewel and the envy of the brother worlds.

Before the city was built, the valley of Huron was discovered. Because of its rich magic, a fierce civil war broke out among all the lings. Humling, creachling, bigling, midgling, faerling. They fought over rights for the valley and its magical properties. As a truce, Rah-Neron the Wise, decided to build the city of Huron. All races were given their own boroughs. It has become a metropolis, a melting pot, if you will, of Möon's fantastic creatur—"

"Forgive me," Daniel interrupted. "Aside from your more interesting rendition of Moon, we would have found evidence of a previous civilization. It's nothing more than a mass of iron and dust."

"Yes. That was before the wars and the burning away of all Möon's creatures. There is no evidence of a previous civilization because what you see in the sky, my friend, is a corpse, the ghost of a once powerful, magical world. Some dark force ripped off the skin between that time in history and today and flung the moon away from Earth to become a satellite, instead of a brother. Even your scientists, Daniel, attest to the fact that Moon is the remnant of a larger, more Earth-like planet."

"Yes, well..." Daniel fell silent.

In fact, everyone else fell silent too, except for the whistling of the pressers.

Nick took a step closer to the stardust. "Home?"

Grand nodded. "That's right, lad."

"They're all like you?" Nick said.

"Well... afraid there is no one like me in Huron. The citizens are more... civilized. But yes, I call them brethren."

"Right," Tim said in a slow, unbelieving tone. "Look. All I care about is Mom and Dad. If these are some type of mimes or clones or whatever scientists call them, where are my parents?"

"They're home. Oxbar Estates, Manor Major, southeast of Huron." Grand pointed to the center of a large continent.

"No. I mean, really, Grand. I'm fourteen already. You don't have to fabricate stories to make me feel better. Where are they *really?*"

"I wouldn't lie to you, Tim. As I said, the trackers hunted us throughout Huron Valley. I left them secured at Manor Major."

Nick looked to the shriveling mimes. "So, they're not my parents?"

"No." Grand shook his head. "Surprised you never suspected. I did a poor job making them, and I'm not trying to be modest either. The trackers were close on our heels, and I had to cut the mime's firing time short by ten minutes. Pulled them out of the kiln too fast, and they cooled immaturely."

"That's why they're so weird," Nick said. "Always acted like they were cool, hip—one of us. Basically teenagers."

"Yes," Grand nodded. "The mimes share your parent's memories; that's one of the first things you add to the brew. But their personalities were underdeveloped."

Phfit. Phfut. Phfit. Phfut.

"But we digress," Grand clasped his hands behind his back and sighed, looking the Lyons brothers dead in the face. "I am ashamed to admit it, but because I abandoned Huron to her own devices, she has abandoned me. I am no longer her steward." Grand's bear-like finger rose to Nick. "You are Nikolas Lyons. She will speak to you now."

"Speak?" Nick said. "Like with words?"

"Yes." Grand pursed his lips. "When the city of Huron was built many epochs ago, a strange thing occurred. A voice from the steward's horn called to Rah-Neron. It was then the settlers learned that every city has a voice. You see, a city contains thousands, even millions, of citizens. If there were no voice, anarchy and death would reign. The voice of the city is a guiding light for all. But she doesn't speak to just anyone. Huron speaks only to her steward, and you, Nikolas, are that steward."

"You're kidding, right?" Tim laughed. "Steward? As in concerned for the well-being of other life forms?"

"Could there be any doubt?" Grand said.

"Ha!" Tim shook his head. "Yes. There could be."

"He's like me in so many ways," Grand said, "if that be an indication of his care for the well-being of others."

In his mind, Nick saw Grand fling an inocudrone across the room and lift two bodies out of a casket.

Really not helping, Grand.

"Yes," Grand said. "He is just like me, right down

to name and place in the family order. The voice is passed down from grandfather to grandson. Always the youngest. You are the youngest, right?"

"Yeah," Tim said. "By twenty-eight minutes, though."

"Always the youngest grandson," Grand said. "And you are named Nikolas Lyons. Every Steward of Huron is given the name, so she might find him. I am Nikolas Lyons, the Eleventh."

"Well, that's a problem, then," Tim said. "His name is Nick. It's on the birth certificate."

"Are you my translator, Tim?" Nick said. "Shut it, already. I can speak just fine."

"It *should* be Nikolas," Grand said. "Your father named you so before we came here. Anyway, that can be rectified. I will take you to the Hall of Pickings so that you might be given your true name." Grand's voice lowered. "It is to you that the stewardship passes. And with it, the voice of Huron. She will speak only to you, Nikolas. That is why I brought you here tonight. The Merrows need you, Nikolas. I must bring you back to your city."

"*I'm* the steward?" Nick said.

Grand nodded slowly. He marched to the truck and lifted the seat, revealing a dozen strange oddities. "There you are." Grand held up a small copper box in both hands, with a cone-shaped tube pointing upward. Clutching the device, he moved back to Nick. "Ask her what she would have us do next."

"What?" Nick said.

"It's a gramophone," Daniel said. "One of the first record players."

"Yes. The gramophone was inspired by the steward's horn." Grand raised the device to Nick. "Ludwig gave it to me so that Huron could speak to you and tell us what to do next. She speaks to her steward through the horn. Nikolas, please."

"So." Nick pulled his hands out of his back pockets. "What do you want me to do?"

"Rub your finger over the surface, like this." Grand glided his fingers over the small rubber pad.

Nick slowly reached out with his hand. Small bits of static leapt to his finger as he pressed down. Then, just like Grand, he rubbed the pad in a circular motion. Garbled murmurs crept from the horn. Nick pressed harder and with more speed. The murmurs shaped into a woman's voice. Huron's voice spoke:

"Steward. Where are you? They come to your city. They bring the smell of death to your streets, to your citizens! Come home, steward. Save your city. Save us from this death!"

"She sounds bummed out," Xanthus said.

Tim huffed. "You don't expect us to buy all thi—"

Grand interrupted Tim and said, "There you have it, Nikolas. So, will you come home? Will you arise and take your place among the clouds?"

Nick looked back at his grandfather. He stood like some giant among the stardust-made planets. Jupiter clung to his shoulder, slowly falling apart among the folds of his trench coat.

Phfit. Phfut. Phfit. Phfut.

Nick's gaze turned toward Moon. According to Grand, it was the ghost of an ancient, magical planet. He'd already been there, hadn't he? There was that strange vision of him standing on the cobblestone streets of Huron. He had that really cool katana in his right hand and was wearing a bowler hat. It felt like home. Maybe that would explain Nick's obsession with the lunar colonies? Maybe Grand's fantastic version of Moon was the home he'd been searching for all along?

Or maybe Grand was completely insane.

Phfit. Phfut. Phfit. Phfut.

Then again, a fairy tale world might not be so bad. Those Grimm fairy tale stories always seemed uncomplicated. You know, big bad wolf, three little pigs, make sure you build your house out of brick kinds of stories. If that's what life on Moon was really like, then that's where he belonged, right? A simple life.

Nick smiled at that idea. He could finally have a simple life. But was that what he really cared about?

Phfit. Phfutt, phfitt. Phfitt. Phfitt, phfutt.

He remembered what truly mattered. He looked back to the Kobayashi brothers and the Wendell sisters, and then down to the leashes scattered at their feet. Caroline's readout blinked: *Life expectancy: 17.* Haley's: *18.* Ever since Nick saw Jermaine hyperventilating on the ground while shoppers marched around him, he only cared about one thing.

"Yes, Grand," Nick nodded. "I will go with you and become this steward. Bu—"

"Very good, Nikolas!" Grand clapped, marching to the truck. "Knew you'd be up for it. Now, we have very little time to l—"

"Wait a second." Nick put a hand up. "Here's the deal. If I go, they go."

"What?" Grand stopped in midstride. "All of them?"

"We're a package deal. I'm taking my friends out of here, or I'm staying with them."

"Our mission is far too dangerous, lad. I cannot allow it."

"Then I stay." Nick crossed his arms. "All I care about is taking care of them. You don't know how they treat refugee kids. They're tagged, Grand. They can't be more than fifteen miles away from the refugee camp before they're shocked by leashes, like a dog. The farther away, the worse it gets."

"Isn't it for their safety?"

"Not even," Nick's voice rose. "The Geneva virus is out of control at the camps. Most of the refugees die before they're eighteen. BioFarms counts on it 'cause they have a contract with the government. Cheaper to harvest organs than to grow them yourself. Leashes make sure the refugees don't run away with their precious property. It's not right, Grand."

"I have seen darkness in my time, but this is un-heard of," Grand said. "Surely the U.S. government wouldn't allow it. Its own citizens?"

Haley sneered, "BioFarms foots the bill, and the government looks the other way. It's considered bio-ethically responsible to pass your organs on, so a few fancy lawyers have their own souls removed and then draft up the legal papers. BioFarms can leash us, brand us, chip us, or whatever else they feel is necessary to protect their assets."

"They come with us," Nick said.

"You're serious, Nikolas. Aren't you?" Caroline said.

"Yes. I am. This is what we've been talking about, right guys? Get away from all the craziness. Huron could be a new home for us?" Nick turned back to his grandfather. "Sorry, Grand, but we're a package deal."

Grand nodded slowly. "It is so. But their very lives are in your hands, Nikolas. *You* are responsible."

"Yeah, of course," Nick realized how non-commit-tal that sounded. "I mean—yes—responsible—I'm responsible."

"Nikolas? Responsible? OK. I'm done with all this." Tim stepped in between Grand and Nick. "When did everyone take a swan dive into Nick's Kool-aid? I'm sorry, Grand. I'm sure you think we're just kids who'd believe any crazy story about tethered worlds and cit-ies that speak to stewards, and that these aren't our parents but just clones you baked in an oven—"

"Actually they're half-baked," Nick snickered.

"Half-baked." Xanthus gave him a fist bump. "Nice one."

"We don't believe you, Grand," Tim continued. "The trackers are just genetic mutations. You're using nano-technology for the dust. And you OD'd on some illegal substance playing World of Witches and Wizards."

"Grand isn't crazy." Nick rounded on Tim. "He's *Grand*. I believe him."

"That's a no-brainer," Tim laughed. "Cause you're like the most naïve person on the planet, Nick. Grand is senile. Look around. Do you think anyone else believes Earth and Moon were lassoed together? By magic? Like some old bedtime story?"

"I do." Caroline poked her hand up.

Xanthus straightened. "There'll definitely be pain involved if someone tries to stop me."

"Really?" Tim said. "Caroline? Xanthus? Really?"

"Did you see those things?" Brandy pointed toward Colorado City. "They ain't from around here."

"I must warn you, though," Grand said. "If you come, Möon carries its own danger."

"It isn't the danger." Haley's hand unconsciously moved over her naked wrist. "It's that we can't protect ourselves from it."

"You will be given the latitude and freedom that comes with youth at your age," Grand said. "I will make you all wards of the House of Lyons."

Haley turned to Brandy and Caroline. "Then, we're going. At least, the Wendells are."

"Come on," Tim said. "Just like that? Daniel?"

Daniel shifted his cane. "Science could only profit from such a trip. Yes, I will go."

"Wha—?" Tim turned to Haley. "Haley? You're not buying this, are you?"

Haley shrugged. "Yeah, I am."

Tim looked shell-shocked. He couldn't believe the Earth and Moon were tethered together in some forgotten, mythical age. On the other hand, Haley did.

"The question isn't to them," Grand said. "The question is to you, Tim Lyons. Will you cross the tether with us? You do not have to go. I can set up an account here. You'll never have to work again."

Tim's mouth hung open. "But, wha—seriously, guys. There's just no way... I mean, you guys can't really think the Moon—" He looked to his friends and then to Haley.

What would Tim choose? Principles were important. Haley's lips were soft and pink.

"Whatever," Tim crumbled.

Grand handed the steward's horn to Nick and collected the pressers. "All right. I've let nostalgia and bygones delay us. Now to the gateway."

"Like a food pantry," Xanthus said, "or, um, wardrobe?"

Grand stopped. "If it were only that easy." He turned and pointed to the sky. "The doorway is right... there."

"In the Great Cloud?" Xanthus said.

"No," Grand said. "*Beyond* the Great Cloud."

"What... space?" Tim said. "*Outer* space?!"

"Yes. Afraid so, Tim."

"Of course," Daniel said. "The gateway is a pre-fabricated wormhole."

"No," Grand said. "Nothing so crude. A wormhole is a tear, a scar in the heavens. This is a passageway made by the hands of a craftsman. And this is the key. It is a chronostone." Grand held up an obsidian stone in his hand. "Quickly now. Colorado Spaceport's west gate is shut down for remodeling. Work crew comes in the morning."

Chapter Fifteen
The Good Life

The air conditioner grumble covered the soft shuffle of seven kids and one middle-aged man slinking their way through the empty halls of the Private Interplanetary Shuttle Station.

"Oh, Mr. Grand, sir," Caroline whispered. "I meant to ask you. Where will we live? Do you rent your own house?"

"I own my own house. In fact, I own Oxbar Estates and all the property that resides therein. Over three hundred acres of land just outside of Huron."

"Does it have a dining room? Like in the old movies?"

"Yes. Five to be exact. Six floors. And a kitchen the size of a tavern."

"So," Brandy waved her hand. "Are there balls and dances and stuff?"

"Coaches studded with diamonds drawn by a flock of geese will escort you to the finest balls in the valley."

Brandy grabbed Caroline's hand, trying not to squeal herself into cardiac arrest.

"Now, I need access to one of the shuttles." Grand slipped out a green card. "Kings will invite you to dinner, but janitors will get you into the storehouse." He raised his eyes, scanning for anything familiar. "Mason Interplanetary Shuttle. Gate B15... Ah, there ya are. Wait here by the counter now. Stay to the ground."

Nick nodded.

"Oh, one other thing Nikolas," Grand said.

"Yeah."

Grand pointed a flashlight at the small obsidian stone in his hand. "I'll need a co-pilot to activate the timeway while I fly the shuttle. May I entrust you with the chronostone to open it?"

"Sure!" Nick caught himself and whispered again. "Sure."

"That's a good lad. I've written the spell on the piece of paper. Once the potion inside is released, it will mix with the sunlight and open the gate."

Nick slipped the chronostone into the pocket of

his khaki shorts.

This all struck him as crazy weird. A magical stone lay at the bottom of his pocket, among some tissues and an old pack of gum. But that wasn't the only crazy weird thing he experienced. It was there when Grand asked him to take his place as steward. And he told Nick he was responsible.

Responsible.

That's something adults usually didn't associate with Nick. And they *definitely* didn't entrust him with powerful magical objects that could open a gateway through space and time. Maybe Nick should tell Grand about all his misadventures that had ended in explosions and fire.

"All right. Need to see about overriding some pass codes to the shuttle. Stay on the ground." Grand moved into the shadows.

Everyone else grunted to their knees and crawled blindly until they found a couple of service counters. Xanthus's hologlasses clicked, flashing two red lights. He reentered the world of *Magicgeddon*.

"Careful, Haley," Tim said. "The counter's right here. Just ten feet in front of you."

"I know that's not your hand touching my hand," Haley warned.

"No." Tim cleared his throat. "No. My hand is not touching your hand."

Haley got up and sat next to Brandy.

"I get it," Tim mumbled to himself. "You're under

the Nick spell."

"Excuse me?" Haley scrunched her face.

"All of you are," Tim sneered. "This has nothing to do with the Geneva virus and living in a big house. You guys are just under the crazy 'Let's do whatever Nick says 'cause he's so cool, even if he tells us to cover ourselves in gasoline and run into a burning building' spell. Might I remind everyone that Nick's ideas end in pain and death? Are you really going to follow him into crazy moon-world 'cause you think he's cool?"

Nick waited for someone to disagree. "Cool" would be the stupidest reason to take a risk like this.

All eyes moved away from Tim.

"See, that's what I thought."

"Hey," Haley snapped her head around.

"What?"

"Shut up, Tim."

Nick heard those familiar motherly sounds of purse straps and flats. "Hey, Caroline."

"Hungry?" Caroline said. Nick's eyes adjusted enough to see Caroline's maternal expression.

"Hungry? I'm a hormonally-induced food receptacle. When am I ever not hungry?" Nick smiled.

"Always with the smiles." She opened her beige purse and fumbled through a jumble of pencils, notepads, and sewing kits. Nick was convinced that in the event of a plane crash Caroline's bag could double as a flotation device.

"Peach, blueberry or chocolate?" Caroline said.

"Um, chocolate."

"Dark chocolate, milk chocolate or white chocolate?"

Nick blinked.

"Have to make sure there are plenty of options for the boys. Daniel really likes white chocolate when he's researching, multi-grain blueberry granola when he's thinking. And Xanthus... well, he just likes to eat. I bet you're a dark chocolate kinda boy?"

"Yeah. *Love* me some dark chocolate."

Without even looking down, she plunged her hands deep in the purse and retrieved a Mr. Good Crunch dark chocolate bar. He grabbed the bar from her hands and tore into it.

"Thanks." Nick's salivary glands were already firing up.

"Tim's into Haley, isn't he?"

Nick thought about blowing off the question, but Caroline wasn't really asking.

"I hope he doesn't get hurt," she said. "Did you hear about the Christopher McCaffrey incident, Nikolas?"

Nick shook his head as the dark chocolate and caramel started to gum up his teeth.

"Christopher McCaffrey lived in perimeter 415. You know, back at the refugee camp. He liked Haley a lot, and I mean a lot. Wrote her a love ballad. Well, actually just played Guitar Champion for her and changed some of the words. I think it was Steellica's

'Wherever I May Roam.' His version was 'My Love is like the Colorado Superdome.' She wasn't very kind to him at all. Or the guitar. Or the pavement."

"I think Tim is just trying to wait her out. You know, wear her down," Nick said, choking down a thick piece of dark chocolate.

Caroline didn't respond immediately. She gingerly peeled the wrapper of a white chocolate bar and broke off a piece just big enough to fit between her fingers. "You don't know her very well. Do you, Nikolas?"

"Sure I do," he said. "People aren't that hard to understand. Haley hates love. Brandy loves fashion. Tim's a wuss. Daniel, evil scientist. Xanthus, dragon nerd. And you, good cook."

Pain flashed behind Caroline's horn-rimmed glasses.

"People aren't cut-outs, you know." She closed her purse.

Nick felt his own stomach bottom out. "I know— I—just, sometimes, we make everything too complicated, you know. Just keep it simple, keep life simple. Why do you think I want to get out of here so bad?"

"Anyway..." Caroline chose to abandon that line of conversation. "I just don't want Tim to get hurt. Haley doesn't know how to let boys like her. I suspect that's why she's into martial arts—to keep boys away. We're from Seattle, you know, and our lives weren't much better before the refugee camp either. My father died in a boating accident when Mom was pregnant with

Brandy. I was two, Nikolas. I don't even remember him. I do remember all of Mom's boyfriends though. Lots and lots of boyfriends. Coffee shop workers, restaurant managers, fishermen. I didn't mind them too much when they weren't drinking, but Haley, well, she hated them all, and hated Mom for having them. Always got into arguments, accusing Mom of choosing her boyfriends over us. Mom said she needed the help, couldn't get through life alone. Mom and Dad married straight out of high school. She won Miss Teen Washington that year, and it was the last job she ever had. Mom was very pretty, you know. They say I have her ears." Caroline paused.

"Um. Nice ears." Nick guessed at the nonverbal cue.

"Thank you very much, Nikolas. Anyway, I made a mistake. I told Haley she looked just like Mom, that she was really pretty and would have all the boyfriends she ever needed. I was twelve then. She was thirteen. Haley was angry, and I think it made Brandy a little jealous, too, which makes sense, if you know Brandy. Anyway, Haley wouldn't talk to me for a month. It would have been longer Nikolas, except that's when Mom died of the virus..."

Caroline's voice trailed off.

"Hmm," she cleared her voice. "Anyway. Just a hint to Tim. Don't try to help her—"

Daniel waved and then pounded the floor. Everyone froze.

A white glow moved from the ceiling to the floor. All heads turned to the counter, looking for the source. A holographic image of a middle-aged woman appeared, followed by a white square box.

"Another nannydrone," Nick groaned.

They did their best to shrivel into the plastic floor.

"Nick?" the nannydrone said.

"Yeah..." Nick said slowly.

"Due to a lack of concern for other life forms and a propensity toward violent behavior, I am to administer the neural inhibitor, R-5235—"

"Aw geez." he pushed himself from the counter.

Suddenly, the drone's head retreated.

"Where did it go?" Brandy said. "What'd you do Nick?"

"I don't know," Nick said. "And I don't ca—" A warm drop of liquid plopped onto Nick's hand. Everyone's eyes moved back to the counter. The nannydrone's face returned, but its body was trapped between a row of canine teeth. The mouth unhinged and squeezed the drone down a pink gullet. Flashing red lights were the last to be seen.

It was a scucca.

Gunk. Gunk. Gunk came the sound of its neck nostrils sniffing. The scucca extended its head over the counter. *REEEIGGHH!!* It called the others.

All three scuccas lifted to their hind legs, and their membrane crowns flicked out.

"The trackers found us," Grand yelled. "To the

shuttle!"

Their grandfather had suddenly appeared holding a massive battle-axe. Where did he get the battle-axe? Nick didn't know, but there were more pressing matters. Like how fast could he make it to the shuttle while maintaining all bodily functions. Everyone flung themselves through the door, down the steps, and onto the tarmac. There, off in the distance, was a lone shuttle titled: "Mason." Nick charged ahead, reached the stairway first, and flew up with his fist aimed for the access button. He punched the *DOOR OPEN* button, but it responded:

Access denied.

Access denied.

Access denied.

Access denied.

"Keycard. Keycard. Grand has it!" Nick turned back to the spaceport. On cue, glass exploded followed by a mass of trench coat and battle-axe flying through the midnight air. Grand tumbled inches from the shuttle. He groaned and fell unconscious.

"Get the card! Grand's keycard. It's green." Nick pointed at Grand. Haley and Xanthus were already trolling through his pockets.

The scuccas fumbled through the opening.

"Here." Haley pressed the card into Nick's shaking hand. He slid it into the key slot.

Beep. Beep. Access granted. Welcome, Mr. Lyons.

"Get inside. Now!" Nick commanded.

Hands grabbed for Grand and the axe. With much heaving and iron scraping, they rolled him through the hatchway and tumbled in themselves. Nick punched the door-closed symbol.

BAAANGH! BAAANGH! BAAANGH! Several bulges punched from the other side of the door. The scuccas were ramming the hull.

"We need to call the police, Nick." Tim said, trying to catch his breath.

Talons started to rake the hull, looking for any sign of weakness.

"Nick?" Haley said, wiping Grand's blood off her cheek. "What are we gonna do?"

BAAANGH! BAAANGH! They rammed again.

"Nick, the police?" Tim said.

Nick scanned the shuttle. Fear was on everyone's face as they listened to three monstrous freaks clawing at the hull. He looked down to his grandfather. He wasn't going to wake up any time soon.

Come on, Grand. Nick thought. *What are we supposed to do?*

"Police, Nick?" Tim said.

Suddenly, Nick understood.

This was all on him.

He got to his feet and looked to the front of the shuttle.

"Police, Nick?" Tim repeated.

"Move." Nick pressed Tim to one side.

"Are you listening to me?"

Control panels lit at the presence of a human. *Hello. Welcome to the Mason.*

BAAANGH! The shuttle rocked.

The control board was a dizzying array of gauges and lights. After a few scans, Nick found a hexagon-shaped disc with a green light emanating from it. He pressed it.

It blinked in red letters: *Access denied. Retinal verification required.* Next to the warning was a small circle with one digital eye.

Nick stood straight, wiping the sweat off his forehead. He looked back at Haley and then Grand. She read his mind. They both picked up Grand by his massive shoulders and lifted him to the retinal scanner. It was strange handling his grandfather's head like some bearded football, but he didn't really have a choice. Nick pried an eyelid open, revealing an unfixed pupil. The retinal system began to scan.

Welcome, Mr. Lyons, to the Mason Transworld Shuttle. Forgive me for asking, but you seem a bit peckish. Are you feeling well this evening? Ibuprofen perhaps?

Grand's chin bobbled to his chest.

BAAANGH! BAAANGH! The scuccas continued to search for the hull's weakness.

"Nick!" Tim yelled. "Are you listening to me? Grand's unconscious or worse. We're trapped. How're we getting out of here?"

Nick tried to subdue the small rise of his cheek, but it was mutinous.

"Hey—Are you smiling?" Tim said. "You're thinking something, Nick."

"I have an idea," Nick said.

"Idea? What do you mean, idea?" Tim took in the scene playing out in front of him. "No!"

"I'm gonna fly it," Nick shrugged.

"No, you're not. Seriously, Nick, you can't fly a *space* shuttle."

"It's easy," Nick said. "I've played *Maverick Seven* like a hundred times. It's an exact replica of this."

"A VIDEO GAME?" Tim said. "You think you're qualified to fly a commercial space shuttle because you played a VIDEO GAME?!"

"Look," Nick said. "Grand told me I was responsible for everyone. I have to do something."

Tim smacked his head. "Where does a fourteen-year-old flying a commercial shuttle fit into *responsible*? Tell him, Daniel. This is insane."

"Yes." Daniel nodded. "I would advise Nick to keep a safe distance from all technological devices, but in this particular situation I am in full support. He has accrued many hours on the holobox, suggesting that he has the skills to fly the shuttle. But I'm not blindly optimistic. I'd say there's a strong chance one of us will die. I would wager that it would be you, Tim. Your heightened fear in an emergency situation like this would lead you to make irrational decisions. And your motor skills are below average for a fourteen-year-old boy. Not to mention you're wearing a red shirt."

"Hey. I'm a human being, not one of your statistics, you freak!" Tim snapped. "And what does the color of my shirt have to do with anything?!"

Nick yelled over Tim, "Maverick Seven? Anyone played? I need a co-pilot."

"I have!" Xanthus sprung from his seat.

"Look. This is real!" Tim banged on the cockpit ceiling. "This isn't a video game or some crazy invention. This is a real GPS! That's a real ion fuel gauge to real ion fuel. And we could all be blown to REAL blubbery, smoldering pieces!"

Everyone yelled in unison, "SHUT UP, TIM!"

"What's your ranking?" Nick said to Xanthus with both hands behind his back.

"Sir, Sergeant General. 5th Class, sir!" Xanthus held a salute.

"Level?"

BAAANGH! BAAANGH! BAAANGH!

Xanthus rocked to his knees, but held his salute. "Sir, Andromeda Mission, sir!"

"You recognize the shuttle then, Sergeant?" Nick nodded to the control panel.

"Sir. This is a Class C, twin ion engine. Full interplanetary travel, but limited interstellar. Stick is a little touchy, sir!"

"All right, co-pilot Kobayashi, take a seat."

Both boys sat down.

"Did you beat the Andromeda mission, Sergeant

General 5th Class?" Tim said.

"Pshh. Dude, not any harder than the Belton level. The landing is always a little interesting."

"Again, I ask. Did you beat it?"

"Security!" Xanthus called.

Haley reached over and pulled Tim into a chokehold. "Let's go, Tim."

"No. No. No. No!" Tim's feet grabbed the doorframe, chairs, shuttle wall, Daniel. Caroline's whispery voice cut through the pandemonium. "Nikolas."

"Yes, Caroline?" Nick looked back.

"We're here because we trust you."

"Thanks."

"Yeah," said Haley, throwing Tim into the back row. "Mom made me promise to look after my kid sisters, so no crashing and burning and screams of death. OK? Promise?"

"Promise." Nick nodded and tapped the passenger door.

"We're all going to d—!" The closing cabin door cut off Tim's screams of death.

"I got this," Nick nodded. "I've beaten the Andromeda level. Twice."

"Really?" Xanthus shouted. "No way! No one beats Andromeda! I got a T-shirt that says it. I am now submitting your name to *Perlock's Mythological Bestiary, 30th edition.* Entry title: Epicness," Xanthus announced while punching several buttons. The shuttle began to slowly rise, pointing its nose skyward.

BAAANGH! BAAANGH! The scuccas continued to hammer away at the hull.

Nick looked to the perimeter cameras. The monsters were crawling around the body, trying to slip their talons into any available crack.

"All right, co-pilot Kobayashi. Systems check complete?"

"Complete. O' Captain."

"The clamps?"

Xanthus had one hand on the seat and another reaching for a blue switch. He turned it and the clamps released, making the shuttle shift.

"All right," Nick announced, "starting initiation sequence now. Ten. Nine. Eight. Seven—"

BAAANGH! BAAANGH! BAAANGH!

"Sixfivefourthreetwoone!" Nick punched the blue launch button.

The boys nodded to each other as the shuttle rumbled to life. A fiery orange skirted the windows, setting off monstrous screams.

"Can fire kill them?" Nick said.

"No. Just slows them down," Xanthus answered.

The shuttle kicked, and both boys squared their sights. The cockpit began to shake, making Nick's teeth rattle.

"OOOHH—MMAA—MAAAN—NN." Xanthus's flabby face was undergoing its own launch sequence. "TT—HHIISSS IISS AAWWWE—SSOS-SOME!"

"And we have lift off." Nick smiled.

Within minutes, they broke through the Great Cloud, and the GPS read five miles altitude. The panel flashed that the launch sequence would end in fifteen seconds, a cue for Nick and Xanthus to take the controls.

"Almost forgot." Nick reached into his khaki pocket and pulled out Grand's chronostone. "The key to the gateway."

Nick put the stone onto his lap, leaned forward, and grabbed the control stick. It felt metallic and cold, nothing like the holobox version. Nick pulled the stick back, but it kicked out of his grip.

"Hey!" He put his hands up.

A holographic man dressed in a captain's outfit sprung from the console. "Welcome to your autopilot, Mr. Steward Lyons. We have already plotted the course uploaded to your keycard."

Xanthus moaned, "Autopilot."

The computer displayed a green line arching from Earth to a white square.

"No!" Nick yelled at the holograph. "We're the pilots. We're supposed to fly it. I hate this planet!"

The shuttle turned a strong left and toward Moon.

The autopilot announced, "Now, sit back, Mr. Lyons, relax, and enjoy one of your favorite singers from the twentieth century: Tony Bennett."

A holograph of Tony Bennett flickered on and began snapping to a beat. "Oooh, the good life. Full of fun, seems to be the ideal…"

"Wow," Xanthus said. "Look at those stars. Never been in space before… Hey, Nick."

"Yeah."

"Back at the church, something weird happened when your grandpa punched the scucca. His eyes were all nuclear reactor blue. His hands, too."

"It's awesome. Grand calls it jynn'us. We all get these mythic powers when we breathe Möon air," Nick said.

"No way!" Xanthus's salami arms punched the air.

"I know, right?" Nick said.

"Don't tease me like that. Are you serious?"

"I'm not kidding. And your jynn'us is supposed to reflect who you are or something. It's gonna be fun on the other side."

"Totally agree… seriously, those are a lot of stars…. Hey, bet I'll get that power where I soak up everyone else's power. But I won't be a villain or nothing. I'll just be like the Sorcerer General over a legion of magical creatures. Yeah. That'd be sweet. Hey, dude. Ten minutes, twelve seconds to vector. Are we supposed to do something?"

"Yeah," Nick said. " Grand gave me a key, but just give me another minute. Need to catch my breath."

"It's the good life, to be free, and explore the unknown," Tony crooned away while the sun's rays escorted them spaceward.

Nick glanced at the perimeter camera. The American continent was completely shrouded by the cloud cover, but more importantly, the scuccas started to slip from the hull. The first two peeled off, and the third was dragged down until it was enveloped by the rocket fire.

Nick's chest deflated, and he said, "They're gone."

He grinned. Had to hand it to himself. They had launched the shuttle, managed to get away from the monsters, and no one had gotten hurt... for the most part. Even if the autopilot took away all the fun, at least they had made it off Earth. Then it hit him. He looked back at Earth and smiled.

I got away.

And it really wasn't all that complicated, Nick thought. *See, Caroline? Life can be simple. Just keep it simple.*

"Oh, the good life," Tony continued to sing. "Let's you hide the sadness you fee—"

"Forgive the interruption." Tony Bennett was replaced by the autopilot. "An uninvited passenger has been detected on the hull."

WHAMM-CRAKK!! The scucca head-butted the cockpit window.

"Woah!" The boys sat up.

The scucca's talons anchored into the shuttle as it studied the two boys. It looked to Nick, to Xanthus, and then to Nick again.

CRAKK!! CRAKK!! CRAKK!! The glass fractured, sending a white thread across the cockpit view.

"Dude! It can't breathe out here," Nick said. "This is OUTER SPACE."

"I know, I know." Xanthus quickly flipped through his bestiary.

CRAKK!! CRAKK!! A dozen more threads shot across the glass.

"It doesn't breathe oxygen." Xanthus held up the bestiary. "It lives on scent!"

"What do you mean, scent? You have to have oxygen to breathe scent."

CRAKK!! CRAKK!! CRAKK!! CRAKK!! Nick's cockpit view was a net of fractured glass.

"Asteroid repellant!" Nick pointed to Xanthus's console. It was common for smaller asteroids and space junk to cross paths with interplanetary shuttles.

CRAKK!! CRAKK!! CRAKK!!

"Right." Xanthus grabbed the asteroid repellant trigger and squeezed. The gun kicked. There was no sound, just a flash of light, and the scucca spinning into the inky void.

The vector sign flashed: *0:53.*

"Uh, fifty-three seconds, dude," Xanthus said. "Where is that gate?"

"The key!" Nick had almost forgotten. "In my lap."

Nick picked up the chronostone and pulled out a piece of paper.

"Oops," he said, holding up the spell, which had somehow wrapped around a stray piece of gum.

Xanthus buried his face in his hands.

"Don't worry. I got this." Nick pulled the piece of paper apart, stretching the gum with it. The spell was partially hidden.

Pa—

Nick started to pull bits of gum off the paper.

Pat—

"Forty-two, forty-one, forty," Xanthus's voice quivered.

A piece tore with the gum.

Pata—

Nick tried to reattach the ripped piece.

Pata—hu—

Patahu.

"Patahu!" Nick grabbed the stone and shouted, "Patahu!"

The chronostone quaked in his hands and began to burn. He dropped it. The stone vibrated, hesitated momentarily, and then glass shattered from within. The cockpit filled with hot, yellow light.

Nick cupped his hands around his face to try and see past the webbed glass. Nothing had changed.

"Do you see anything over there?" Nick said.

"No, dude," Xanthus said. "No expanding vortex. No epic, magical gate. Nothing."

"Come on, Grand," Nick groaned.

"Nick," Xanthus said, "your grandpa *is* nuts, isn't he? We're dead! We're all dead! The navigation system says we can't go back now. Not enough fuel. I never even got to kiss Caroline on the mouth."

Nick turned slowly to Xanthus.

"What? I know you guys think I'm this child prodigy of mythological creatures, but I need love, too!"

Nick's eyes fell on the trash chute just below Xanthus's leg.

"Waitasecond!" Nick said. "These shuttles are lined with a UV shield. Grand said the stone interacted with solar light. We have to get the stone outside."

The chute slid open at the presence of Nick's hand, and he shoved the chronostone down. They heard rock scraping through the garbage chute. Metal screamed, and the shuttle kicked from the rear. The stone was free.

A reddish wave rolled over the shuttle.

"Wow," Xanthus said.

"That's a good sign, right, Nick?" Haley's voice crackled over the intercom.

"It's the gateway. Strap yourselves in."

A shimmering pocket materialized into a bright conical object. Its walls were lined with thousands of red stones spinning into a magma center. For all Nick knew, the gateway was the building block of the universe, ready to crush the ship into light and heat. They were about to find out.

"Here we go..." someone said over the intercom.

Tony Bennett extended his hands. "Well, just wake up. Kiss the good life, goodbye."

Kevin Rayfield McGill

Chapter Sixteen
Mermaids!

They were thrown out of a bloom of red fire.

"Did it work?" Haley's voice faded away and then returned. "That's awesome! Are you guys seeing this?"

Xanthus and Nick gasped. Grand's stardust rendering had nothing on the real Möon and Earth.

"Are you seeing this, Nick?" Haley repeated. Brandy and Caroline squealed from somewhere in the background.

"Yeah," Nick said. "'There is another world, but it is in this one.'"

It was Xanthus's turn to look at Nick.

"Yeats," Nick said.

The brother planets were anything but peaceable. Möon hung over Earth, recalling images of Atlas bearing the weight of an entire planet. The sun cast a paternal light between the two weather systems, revealing a black mass of cloud and dust. Lightning crackled between the planets, revealing the tether.

It was the unreal beauty of Möon that made Nick unbuckle his harness and crawl over Xanthus. Scattered underneath the clouds were islands, craggy and desperate. The continents were covered in ripples of mountains that smoothed into deep valleys. The landmasses were utterly blanketed in wild vegetation. There might be cities down there, but Nick couldn't see them.

It looked nothing like his Moon.

"Are you guys getting this?" Tim said.

"Yeah," Nick said. "All of it."

"Please remain in your seats as we begin our descent to Earth's Keranu Wall," the autopilot announced. The shuttle took a sharp right from Möon and steered directly to Earth.

"Wait," Xanthus said. "We're not supposed to land on Earth. We're going to Huron, I thought?"

"I don't know." Nick buckled himself in. "We'll see, I guess."

The shuttle nosed toward Earth's atmosphere. Belts of clouds were the only thing they could see for several minutes until they hit atmosphere. The stars disappeared under steam and fire. Finally, they passed through the cloud line, revealing a swampy landscape with a circle of stone crowning the tether. On a closer look, the tether seemed to be organic, even tree-like. Well, aside from the fact that trees don't grow to the size of mountains.

"I think that's the Keranu Wall," Xanthus said.

"Landing sequence initiated," announced the autopilot.

Suddenly, a gray object flashed by. Before Nick could make out what it was, wind punched through the cockpit and sprayed glass everywhere.

"Hold on to something!" Nick yelled to the intercom. "We've been hit! Something blew out the windshield. Prepare for a crash landing."

The space shuttle flipped over, turning cloud and Earth into a kaleidoscope. After a few rotations, the shuttle stopped tumbling and fell into a corkscrew.

"Sorry, Caroline," Nick said to himself.

The passenger door whipped open, revealing a very confused Grand. He leapt for the controls.

"Autopilot overridden. Emergency landing sequence initiated," the autopilot announced.

After a few grunts and curses, Grand leveled the shuttle. Nick heard the small blast of air and two parachutes opening from the wings.

Too late.

The shuttle slammed ground, skipping over rocks and bushes. Tree limbs shredded the parachutes. Branches slapped the window. Rocks scrapped the bottom, and muddy water sprayed over the windshield. They slid for what seemed like an eternity until a tuft of land kicked them to a stop. Grass and dirt flicked upward and then rained down in thick, muddy plops.

"Welcome to the south side of the Keranu Wall," announced the computer.

Grand's quivering brow set on Nick. A ribbon of blood ran around his eyes, down his cheek, and across his chest. He breathed deeply and roared, "Well done, Nikolas! There's my copilot."

"That was awesome!" Nick stood to his feet, adrenaline still pumping through him. "We were, like, spinning, and then the parachute, and then we just rammed into the ground."

"Something hit us?" Xanthus said.

"You mean those?" Grand pointed to the tether. "Groungers."

Several winged tadpoles the size of a small plane swarmed the tether. Electricity threaded through their bodies, lighting up a mangle of intestines and bones.

"Groungers?" Xanthus said. "Those aren't in my bestiary."

"They feed off the tether's electricity. The shuttle's power system was just another meal."

Grand stood full height, let out a triumphant breath, and stepped into the cabin door. "How are we? Appendages connected to their traditional counterparts?"

Most said, "Yes."

"Good, good," Grand said. "Then we make for Huron, by way of the Mottle Craw."

"Wait," Caroline said. "Shouldn't we rest up? Maybe eat or something? We did just crash land, you know."

"Impossible, Miss Wendell," Grand said. "If we miss this flight, the next won't be for a month. The Merrows need us. Huron cannot wait."

Grand fisted the shuttle door button. *Beep, beep.* The air hissed. Harnesses unclicked, and feet banged through the cabin.

"Why didn't we just land on Möon in the first place?" asked Xanthus. "Would've saved all the screaming and flames of death."

"Couldn't," Grand said. "Möon guards its skies from illegal Earthlings sneaking across. They'd burn us alive before we touched the clouds."

They all piled up around the cabin door to get a view of the outside, except for Tim. He was white knuckling the back of a seat.

"Nothing blew up, Tim," Nick said. "We made it."

"Is there a bathroom on this shuttle?" Tim stood up carefully. "I really hope there's a bathroom on this shuttle."

Nick didn't bother to answer Tim. He was too busy gawking at the scenery. Mud and fog was *everywhere.*

They had landed in a bowl-shaped valley. Trees with no sense of direction climbed out of rock-faces and brackish pools. Where there weren't moldy leaves, mud pockmarked the ground. And where there weren't moldy leaves and pockmarked mud, there were small bits of grass pushing out like upside down goatees. On the cliffsides were several winged ships that looked like they'd been hung out to dry. Each ship had a shabby ladder filled with a long line of odd, malformed-looking creatures and people.

Still, there was mud. Everywhere.

"Earth. Epochs ago," Grand announced, hopping out into a slab of mud.

Xanthus put a hand to his chest and took a ceremonial step into the mud. "Oh wow, wow, wow. Here I step, Xanthus Kobayashi. The first boy to touch foot upon this here ancient and magical Earth.

"Mr. Grand. Have I got questions for you. First let's talk about drago—cawk! Cawk! Cawk!"

Before Xanthus could launch into his questions, he started hacking and coughing.

"I got some questions, too!" Nick gagged. "Like, what's that smell?" The air was rank with a filthy, iron stench.

"That—" Grand's nostrils whistled. "—smells like dirt."

"It smells disgusting!" Brandy covered her mouth with a black silk handkerchief.

"Come now," Grand said. "They have dirt where you're from."

"Not in the cities," Daniel said, covering his own

mouth. "It's synthetic dirt. Meant to keep the germs out."

Mud wasn't the only invasion to their senses. Small little creatures bizzed and buzzed everywhere.

"Are those... ?" Brandy said.

"Yes, Brandy." Daniel steadied himself. "Insects. I've seen them once before, in that museum near Rollhill Pass."

"First, I gotta ask, Mr. Grand, dude," Xanthus said, regaining his senses. "Are Furies benevolent or not? I've always been partial to the anti-hero camp, 'cause, you know, they seek justice, but they're pretty psychotic about it. Like Marvel's The Punisher. Second, and this is really important. Are any of Tolkein's creatures actually real? I hope that's the case. Maybe an Ent, perhaps? Fimbrethil the Ent? But I'll settle for a gollum. Also, are gumnut babies and chucklebuds the same creature? There's been a raging debate on the Myth-us boards for, well... as long as I've been alive. To give my two cents, I would say they were the same creature at one point in history, but a mage or a wizard got involved and created a second species. I'd say the chucklebuds were the original. Kinda like mogwai and gremlins."

Haley and Tim were the last ones out of the shuttle. On the very last step, Haley missed a rung and stumbled to the ground.

"Haley!" Tim yelled.

She tried to pull herself up. "Just—motion sickness. I get it sometimes."

"You need to sit down," Tim insisted. "Just for a minute. Let me help you."

"I'm OK, Tim. Just need to catch my breath." Haley put her hand up, proving she could stand on her own.

Tim ignored her and grabbed her arm.

"Seriously, Tim." Haley's fingers formed into a karate defense position. "Step away."

"Everything all right?" Grand shouted back.

Haley answered weakly, "I'm—just—"

"She gets motion sickness sometimes." Caroline helped Haley to her feet.

"Right," Haley said. "Motion sickness."

"It's the smell!" Brandy said, wrinkling her nose. "She can't stand it. It's making *me* all pukey." She curled her lip as she toed the mud with her Louboutins, shivered, and then retrieved a small bottle of hand sanitizer from her black purse. She lathered it all over her neck, arms and legs. Closing her eyes, she lifted another glop to her face. She tucked the bottle between her arms. "Probably don't even have soap here."

She tossed the hand sanitizer to Caroline, who squeezed out a smaller glop onto her right hand. "Now, Brandy, I'm sure they have soap. What kind of a pl—"

Whheeeeboooom!

Caroline screamed, dropped the sanitizer in the

mud, and raised her arm to shield herself from the mushroom of fire and shrapnel. After a moment, the white-hot cloud settled, leaving behind a burning space shuttle.

"Sorry!" Nick yelled to Caroline over the flames. "I really tried not to blow stuff up."

"Well," She looked back to Nick, yelling over the fiery shuttle, "you didn't blow *us* up, so technically, you kept your promise."

"My bestiary," Xanthus said, reaching into the flames. "My hologlasses!"

Grand grabbed Xanthus by his collar. "Nothing in there you need."

"This is unacceptable!" Xanthus protested. "I have spent the better part of my teen career beating *Magicgeddon*. I need my escape, man."

Grand looked up to Möon and the great tether. "I suppose twin planets tethered together by a magical rope in the distant past will have to do, then. Won't it?"

Xanthus looked up. "Huh. Yeah."

"Let's get moving," Grand said. "Our ship waits for no one."

"OK," Xanthus said. "But I got like a ton more questions for you, Mr. Grand. Minotaurs. Are their hooves split or not? 'Cause..."

And so began their long march toward the Mottle Craw. They were escorted by the sound of muddy footfalls. Daniel's cane *presshed* into the mud while sneakers and black dress shoes *prushed* and *ploshed*. That is, except for Brandy's. She made Xanthus give her a piggy back ride because she wouldn't dare subject her Louboutins to *that* filth.

The conversation fell into smaller factions. Some talked about the strange smells, others commented on the winged-ships in the distance. Brandy polled the group, asking who had the girliest scream when they crash landed. Tim won that prize. But one of them didn't participate in the conversations: Haley. Nick noticed her unsteady stride. But it wasn't just that. Her golden blond hair had gone limp and stringy. He moved closer to ask if she was all right. She waved him off.

They walked for at least another hour. By this time, Xanthus had switched from conversations about mythological body types to a diatribe on why he believed dragon lore originated in China, and not Europe. *Everyone* believed dragons were from England, which was clearly a Eurocentric idea. He then began to list several other creatures that predated European mythology. That was about the time Haley lunged for Nick.

"Haley?!" Nick caught her. "Are you OK? Hey—your eyes!"

Dark circles hung under her blue eyes, and parts of her skin were covered with a creamy, bluish film.

"Just—motion sickness. I get it sometimes." Haley tried to pull herself up. "I'm OK, Nick. Just a little tired." She put her hands up, proving she could stand on her own.

Unaware of the scene behind him, Grand marched on. "Hey!" Xanthus said. "What's with those guys?"

"The swayers?" Brandy said.

"Yeah. Look," Xanthus said, "see, over there. A ton of people standing around those stone pillars, holding their hands up like they're praying to the tether or something."

The circle of pillars looked familiar to Nick. Something about stone circles... Nick laughed, "That's Stonehenge, isn't it Grand."

"I believe it is," Grand said. "But for them it's the Möoncircle."

"Yeah, ok. But you still haven't told us what they're doing," Xanthus said.

Brandy slipped off Xanthus's back to have a better look. She shrugged, "Probably some religious stuff."

"Not religious," Grand said. "They hope to breathe in Möon air. Find their inner-air."

Everyone turned to Grand with a puzzled expression.

"I've got a lot to catch you up on, I see. Earth has little magic, but Möon is filled with it. Its very air is rife with power. The swayers stand on the wall to catch a bit of Möon air."

"What's it doing for them?" Brandy said.

"To begin with, it will extend your life tenfold."

"Tenfold? How old *are* you?" Daniel tilted over his cane.

"Five-hundred and twenty-three."

"Geez," Nick said. "Holding up well, Grand."

"You cannot be that old." Daniel's mouth hung open. "It is... impossible."

"I am, laddie." Grand chuckled. "One doesn't forget five-hundred and twenty-three years. But more importantly, Möon air gives you jynn'us. These poor souls don't need to stand so close to the tether and risk being struck by lightning. This entire valley holds enough deep air to awaken any power they might have."

"Oh yeah. That's another question," Xanthus said. "Can you give me some of that jynn'us?"

"Let's not be hasty, lad," Grand said. "You cannot *get* jynn'us. Magic has a mind of its own. It will choose you if it so desires. And the jynn'us may not always be to your liking. There are a variety of powers for a variety of souls."

"OK." nodded Xanthus. "Variety of powers. I can live with that. So what are my options?"

"There are many options," Grand said. "Trinkes, automa, atla—that one is mine, by the way. Those are the conventional ones. There's also lustratio, transe, ethereal. Thousands really. And new ones crop up everyday. But this is all irrelevant at the moment, Xanthus. It will be months before you'd undergo the transformation."

Xanthus tilted his head. "Is there any way to speed it up?"

Behind the throng of questions, Nick noticed Haley looking to the Keranu Wall. Her head swayed unsteadily, and the blue film had now covered every part of her skin. She was absolutely disinterested in their conversation on jynn'us. No, more than that. It looked like she was about to—

"Eeeewww!" Brandy hopped on one leg. "Not on the shoes! Uggh! You did not just blow chunks all over my Louboutins."

Haley clutched Caroline's arm, trying not to collapse again.

Grand moved around Caroline and gently placed a hand on Haley's shoulder. "Lass. Look at me."

She slowly raised her face to Grand's. The blue film had now covered her hair and teeth.

"I see everything." She squeezed her eyes shut. "It hurts to look. I can see it all."

Grand shook his head and looked to Xanthus. "Afraid I owe you an apology, Mr. Kobayashi."

Caroline cooed as she wrapped her arm around Haley and found a lone boulder. She directed her horn-rimmed glasses to Grand. "What's wrong with her, Mr. Lyons?"

"Everything! Everything is wrong with her, but that will change soon enough," Grand grinned. "Jynn'us has found Haley and within only an hour of our landing. Quite extraordinary."

"No way, Haley!" Xanthus cried. "You got some jynn'us? Already?! I love this place! OK, OK. I gotta record everything that happens to you. And... I need samples. Lots of samples. Hair. Skin. Urine."

"That is disgusting, Xanthus," Caroline said.

"This is a momentous occasion!" Xanthus raised his hands in the air. "You're so lucky, Haley. Oh, wait. You breathe it in, right? Maybe I just need to breathe deeper. You know, open up my lung capacity." Xanthus went bug-eyed, inhaling like a gorilla suffering from cardiac arrest.

Without warning, Grand began to march again. "She will be sick over the next few days. Lucky for you, we have proper quarters on the Mottle Craw, that is, if we make our departure time."

"Ugh." Brandy smacked her shoes on a rock. "Sounds about right. Haley gets a power up, and I'm scrubbing chunks off my shoes."

The valley quickly descended into a thick grove of gnarled trees. It was covered in some kind of sap that was runny and got into everyone's hair. The second it hit their heads, it would crystallize. Everyone started to walk more slowly as they tried to pick the dried sap out of their scalp, ears, and face. It took another hour of spongy bogs, unrelenting rocks, and piggy-back rides, but they finally made it out of the grove and to a field separating them from the cliffside.

Before they knew it, a winged ship fell out of the

sky, hurtling toward them. Everyone but Grand dove to the ground. At the last minute, it turned direction and curled upward. The grass rolled, sticks kicking up.

"OK, that's sweet," Nick said.

"It an aero," Grand said, "our ride to Huron."

It looked like one of those old ships from a pirate movie. Maybe a Spanish galleon? Nick thought.

The winged ship angled up and toward the massive tether in the distance. One could see dozens of other aero ships circling the tether, like hawks around a prey. One by one, the tornado winds pulled the aeros into the sky and toward outer space.

And then he realized something more important.

That was a flying ship!

He was *literally* looking at a real flying ship. This was like some fairy tale. He'd made the right call in believing Grand. And now this was happily ever after. He half expected those words to pop up: 'And they lived happily ever after.' A fairy tale ending. Everything he'd ever wanted.

I made it. WE made it.

Nick let the words tumble out as he clapped his hands, "We made it!"

They all stopped and responded with: "Huh?" and "What?"

"This is what we've always wanted, right? To get away. Find a new life."

Nick waited for some kind of agreement. Their expressions were blank. He jumped to the front of the group.

"Look. You all escaped the refugee camp, we beat those trackers, flew the shuttle all the way here, and now we're about to start our new lives in the cradle of all magical civilization! This is it. Finally. We beat the crazy."

Daniel had no response, which was to be expected, but Caroline's cheeks nudged her glasses as she smiled openly, and Xanthus rocked his head in agreement. Nick couldn't read Grand's face—it was guarded. But adults rarely expressed what they felt anyway.

"And you didn't have to light a tree on fire to do it," Brandy added. "So I call that a win."

"Seriously, people!" Nick shook his hands. "I've never burned down a tree in my life."

"Only cause the pyrodrones were assigned to our house, 24/7," Tim said.

"Anyway," Nick said. "We're here. All I have to do is go to Huron, send help to the Merrows, and we're done. Simple."

"Simple?" Daniel said.

"Yeah," Nick said. "Just like that. Simple! The end! Stick around for the post-credit scene! Refill your popcorn before you leave!" He pointed toward the cliff and commanded, "Let's go!" He knew the command was a bit over the top, but at the moment he was feeling invincible. They'd made it off Earth.

Xanthus called after Nick, "Would it be too meta

if I quoted Samwise Gamgee's line about living out our story?"

Without waiting for an answer, he tried for his best middle-earth accent, which was immediately met with groans: "'Still, I wonder if we shall ever be put into songs or tales. We're in one, of course, but I mean: put into words, you know, told by the fireside, or read out of a great big book with red and black letters, years and years afterwards. And people will say: "Let's hear about Frodo and the Ring!'

"Then Frodo says: ''Why, Sam,' he said, 'to hear you somehow makes me as merry as if the story was already written. But you've left out one of the chief characters: Samwise the stouthearted. "I want to hear more about Sam, dad. Why didn't they put in more of his talk, dad? That's what I like, it makes me laugh. And Frodo wouldn't have got far without Sam, would he, dad?'"

'Now, Mr. Frodo,' said Sam, 'you shouldn't make fun. I was serious.'

'So was I,' said Frodo, 'and so I am.'"

The last leg of Nick and Company's journey went by quickly. For the next twenty minutes they bantered about their new life on a fantastic moonland. Nick was the first to stop directly in front of the cliff. He looked left and then right. All along the cliff face aero-ships were hanging on the sides, just like they'd seen earlier that afternoon. Wooden staircases led up to the ships. The stairs were filled with hundreds of people in line to board.

"We have to wait in those lines?" Haley groaned.

Grand quickly explained that prepaid passengers didn't have to wait. He pointed to something that looked like a giant gourd shell.

"It's a willy-kirk," he said.

The large bowl had grown out of an equally large root. It reminded Nick of an oversized pumpkin attached to a vine. "It'll take us up to our ship. I've never been too good with these willy-kirks though. They require a more delicate touch." He petted the side of the bowl. It shook like a wet cat and tipped over. "Will you look at that? It responded right away. Too much of your Earth's moisturizing soap, I'd wager."

They all stepped slowly into the strange willy-kirk plant. Nick wondered if a bug felt like this as it slowly crawled into a Venus flytrap. When everyone was in, the bowl righted itself and rose skyward, toward the Mottle Craw. Xanthus peered over to see what mechanism was raising them up. He looked at Nick, grinned, and then peered back over. A mechanical lift wasn't raising them up, rather the willy-kirk's large vine.

Satisfied, Xanthus faced the stairway running up the cliff face and began reviewing all the strange creatures. "Gaban, Salk, Centaur... Wait, I know that one. I know it..." He reached into his vest but then remembered that his bestiary had gone up in flames with the shuttle. "A tragedy... Mr. Grand, dude. Are they coming with us?"

"If fate wills it," Grand shook his head. "They're standing in line for the lottery. It is a privilege to go Möonside. You'll find that people will do all sorts of tricks to cross the tether. I once met a fell—"

"Mermaids!" Xanthus cut Grand off and flung himself to the other end of the willy-kirk. Below them another willy-kirk carried two mermen in wheelchairs. "Wicked cool."

Huron's voice knifed Nick's skull: *The Rones lie about their true intent. They enter the city of Huron at the peril of us all!*

Nick grabbed the edge of the willy-kirk.

The Rones lie about their true intent. They enter the city of Huron at the peril of us all.

Nick crumpled to his knees.

"Nikolas?" Grand looked to his grandson.

"It's her..." he tried to stand up.

The Rones lie about their true intent. They enter the city of Huron at the peril of us all.

Nick moaned and wiped something warm from his lip.

Blood.

"What's going on, Grand?" Nick said.

"Is it her?" Grand whispered over his shoulder. "Is Huron speaking to you?"

"She just keeps repeating herself. Goes on and on about those Rones."

"Rones!" Grand shouted, disbelievingly. "Did you say *Rones?*"

"Yeah," Nick nodded. "That's been her message to me the entire time. Inside my head."

Grand grabbed Nick's shoulder a little to hard but he tried to pretend it didn't hurt. "How long have you been hearing from her, and that she's been warning you of the Rones?"

"I don't know," Nick shrugged. "A couple of days before you showed up."

"Oh, Nikolas," Grand shook his head. "Why didn't you tell me she'd been speaking to you, and about the Rones of all things?"

"I forgot. It's been a little crazy lately. Why? What's the big deal?"

"Mermaids, Mr. Grand," Xanthus shouted, pointing to the willy-kirk below them.

"Merrows, Mr. Kobayashi," Grand called back. "That is what we call them. Even so, it isn't their truest name. In more ancient times, they were called something else." Grand looked back to Nick. "Rones."

"Rones?" Nick turned slowly and edged over the willy-kirk. "So, the Merrows lie about their true intent, *they* enter the city of Huron at the peril of us all? Merrows are Rones?"

"One and the same," Grand sighed heavily. "Huron knows the ancient tongue better than our own. Nikolas, she warns you of the evil that the Merrows bring to her city."

Nick shook his head. "What? She—what?"

"Ludwig sent the memory-in-a-bottle to summon you back because he thought the Merrows were in grave danger," Grand said. "He didn't know they were deceiving us.

"Nikolas, Huron didn't call you to save the Merrows. She called you to *stop* them."

Nick watched the older merman adjust his fishtail and pat down his powdered wig. Then he understood.

Life for him and his friends wasn't going to be so simple.

"Everything got complicated, didn't it, Grand?" he said, dropping his chin to the edge of the willy-kirk.

"Yes, lad," Grand said, putting a comforting hand on his shoulder. "I'm afraid your troubles have just begun."

Nick stared at the pudgy merman for another moment and then let out a long, tired sigh.

Made in the USA
Middletown, DE
25 October 2017